THE
CHALLENGE

TOM HOYLE

MACMILLAN CHILDREN'S BOOKS

First published 2017 by Macmillan Children's Books
an imprint of Pan Macmillan
20 New Wharf Road, London N1 9RR
Associated companies throughout the world
www.panmacmillan.com

ISBN 978-1-4472-8677-6

1 3 5 7 9 8 6 4 2

A CIP catalogue record for this book is available from
the British Library.

Printed and bound by CPI Group (UK) Ltd, Croydon CR0 4YY

THE CHALLENGE

Ben's best friend has been found dead after mysteriously disappearing from outside his house. Ben has never felt so alone, until twins Sam and Jack arrive at school and introduce him to The Challenge.

What first seems to be a harmless popularity contest quickly turns sinister. But once you're involved with The Challenge, it's very hard to get out . . .

Books by Tom Hoyle

Thirteen

Spiders

Survivor

The Challenge

To my family

ONE WEEK TO GO

📝 Draft Email

To:	
Cc:	
Subject:	

Someone else has to know the whole truth.

'Christmas Eve, 2016. The middle of London, next to Big Ben. Midday,' he said. Then I watched him disappear into the woodland. With anyone else, they'd be empty words.

It was so far in the future I thought we'd never get here.

I came close to |

Attachment

MAY 2011 – SEPTEMBER 2011 LIFE AFTER WILL: LIFE WITH THE TWINS

My story begins when I was fifteen years old. It was May 2011, a Saturday, 4.45 p.m., immediately after the FA Cup final. It begins the moment I spun the back wheel of my bike and sprayed wet mud across the road.

Bullseye, the dog belonging to Mike, who lived opposite, stood in his open gate and howled. Will swore at me as he wiped specks off his T-shirt.

Will Capling. We had grown up together, our houses more or less opposite one another.

'Hey – where's my hoodie? Have you got it? Thief!' Will's favourite jumper was blue with white strings. If I hadn't splattered his T-shirt with mud, maybe he wouldn't have thought of his jumper.

'You left it in my room, you muppet. You just sit there while I'll get it,' I said as I ran inside. I glanced behind once, and saw Will circling in the road on his bike, one hand on his mobile phone.

Bullseye barked.

2

'Benny, when you come back, I need to tell you something,' Will shouted. Those were his last words. They were possibly his last words *ever*.

The very last time I saw Will Capling, he was playing on his bike in the road.

That was a line from my statement.

'I need to tell you something,' he'd said.

He never had a chance to tell me what.

Thousands of times afterwards, I reconstructed the scene, straining for details. Was there someone in the distance? The sound of a passing car? Anyone? Anything?

I took the stairs two at a time and shouted to my gran: 'I'm just grabbing Will's hoodie. It doesn't feel as warm today.'

I couldn't have been inside for more than ninety seconds, but in that time Will disappeared.

It was a while before I realized something terrible had happened. 'Will, where are you?' I shouted as I came back out into the lane. I rode hundreds of yards in both directions, up and down the road, Will's hoodie tied round my neck, telling him to stop messing about. Then my voice gradually rose: 'Will – don't be a prat! Will? William!' William was what his mum called him.

Bullseye barked again.

I hate the memory of what happened next. I shouted and walked into Will's place. I didn't knock – that's how close we were. My life flowed in and out of their house.

It was half an hour before we started to think something had gone wrong. It was two hours before Will's dad called the police. I remember going to Will's room, folding the hoodie, laying it on his bed. So much of my life had revolved around Will, another only child, the only other boy in a tiny village. When he was taken away, my life was ripped apart.

I was different after Will died. I locked the door to my bedroom; sometimes I also put a chair against it in case an intruder magically slid the bolt across. Maybe I thought whoever murdered Will was going to attack me. Maybe I was worried that Will wasn't around to look after me any more.

The nightmares came: pleas carried by the wind that howled across the Lake; a monster that crawled among reeds and gravestones; faces that yelled at me from underwater, bubbles erupting from their mouths. I was different, withdrawn. Some said I had changed because I'd lost my only close friend, others that I believed it could have been me. I suppose I thought that Will was the better looking one, the funnier one, the sportier one, and felt I wasn't worth as much without him.

As the rest of term passed after Will died – June slipping into July, and a lost, empty summer ahead – sympathy evaporated as people began to forget about Will. Plans for the 'Will Capling Pond' had been put on hold and the new 'Will Capling Cup for Character' was already in danger of becoming another unnecessary prize at the end of term.

I remember one lesson about future careers, when we had to write down what other people thought of us.

Darren Foss, on the table next to mine, put his hand up. 'Benny wants to know how to spell "weird",' he said. Then, 'Benny wants to know how to spell "arse-rash".' Everyone laughed. The teacher just told him to be quiet.

The Twins arrived on the first day of the new school year in September 2011 and changed everything. The first day of The Twins was Day One. Of the 6,000 days of my life, more happened in 100 days with The Twins than in all those days before. Even the days with Will.

The Twins. Sam and Jack. And everyone *said* 'Sam and Jack', never the other way round. Sam was older by a few minutes and he seemed to be the one who made the decisions when they couldn't agree. They were identical, absolutely indistinguishable – not a mole, an eyelash, or an interest that was different – the same liquid poured into two identical pots.

On that first day, I had gone into the toilets and couldn't turn around in time after spotting Darren and a couple of his mates standing between the urinals and basins. I diverted to the cubicles, but a foot appeared in the door just before it closed.

'Aren't you in the wrong room?' said Darren.

'What?' I said, hating myself for having come in while they were around. They had caught me in the same toilets near the end of the previous term and forced my head into the bowl and flushed. Afterwards, I had cried and felt sick, but not because of the physical bullying: for years, Darren had called me 'Will's shadow'; now he thought it was funny to say I was 'a shadow without a body'. It was hard to hide how much that hurt.

'You should be next door with the girls,' he said, mates peering over his shoulder. 'I suppose you're in here because you need to sit down to piss.' They laughed.

I didn't know what to say. That was always the problem. All those words on a page, a top-of-the-class brain, but I couldn't string a few words together.

Darren grabbed my neck with one hand and whipped a pack of cards from my pocket with the other. He tipped them over the floor. I looked down and saw four jacks and four kings scattered around my feet, all the other cards face down. I know the chances of that happening are microscopic, and I don't believe in signs. Maybe I only noticed those cards.

Then I heard a confident voice. 'Can we help in there?' It was the first time I had ever seen The Twins. I think it was Sam. I hadn't heard them enter. I wasn't sure whether they were talking to Darren or me.

'Hey, man,' Darren said, looking from one identical face to the other. 'He's all yours.' Darren turned to leave but The Twins were shoulder to shoulder, blocking his way out of the cubicle, as well as trapping me inside. Darren's mates slunk away without a word – I heard a burst of chatter from outside as the door opened and closed. The four of us stood still.

Jack – and I know it was him because he had 'JT' – Jack Thatcher – embroidered on his shirt – stuck out one finger and gently pressed it to Darren's upper chest. Jack's brown, almost ginger hair flopped down over his ears. Light reflected off his deep brown eyes. He smiled calmly.

I waited for an onslaught from Darren, but nothing came.

'What's your name?' Sam – 'ST' embroidered on his shirt – asked me.

'I'm B-Ben,' I stammered. I had never called myself Ben before; it had always been Benny, or sometimes Benedict.

'Ben,' Sam said calmly, 'I know we're going to be great friends. See you later.' *I know we're going to be great friends*: it was the sort of precise thing The Twins would say. Not *I hope we're going to be friends*. Absolute certainty.

I squeezed between Darren and The Twins, and left as quickly as I could. No sooner had I stepped into the corridor than the bell went. I stood at the corner, just beyond the last locker, waiting for the blue toilet door to open.

Two minutes later, The Twins strode out, chatting casually, heading in my direction, offering me a full deck of cards. 'Hey, Ben,' said Jack. 'We'll see you around.'

I waved the cards at them and smiled. 'Yeah. That'd be great. Any time. Thanks. Really. Thanks.' I sounded desperate, pathetic.

'Maybe tomorrow break-time?' said Sam. He smiled and flicked back hair that was getting close to his right eye. 'You seem pretty cool.'

He was totally convincing, though no one had ever called me 'cool' before (well, my gran genuinely thought I was cool, but she was not a good judge).

'Yeah. Great.' I nodded and grinned, probably giggling a little, but they gave no sign that I was embarrassing myself.

Darren still hadn't emerged from the toilet.

The Twins saw me staring at the door and smiled at each another.

'We just . . .' said one.

'. . . helped him understand,' said the other.

SEPTEMBER 2011
ANGELS

Most people would think it's *impossible* that they charmed everyone from the start, but that's only because you didn't meet Sam and Jack. Being identical twins made them interesting, but it was *much* more than that.

On Day Two, I saw them at break. I was with Blake. Blake had somehow been left behind after friendships were formed. He was gangly and poorly coordinated; he wore thick glasses and had a squeaky voice. He was like a cartoon nerd. We were bonded by the fact that, along with three or four girls, we aced our summer exams. It would have been better if the other boy to do that *hadn't* been Blake – but I was grateful for his company after Will died. Anyway, Blake and I stood on the sideline together and watched the football, mainly because I had spotted The Twins, though I didn't mention that to Blake. I toyed with a pack of cards and Blake pestered me about tricks.

I did have one hobby: magic. It made other people fade into the background, helped me feel strong. Gran had told me that Grandad used to do some magic. And that's another thing that made me different: being brought up by your grandmother. 'His mother died in childbirth' sounds Victorian. Not knowing who your father is sounds twenty-first century.

I couldn't tell which Twin was which, but it was obvious that Sam was the best player on one side and Jack the best on the other. They were even better than the school captain, Head Boy and golden boy, Mark Roberts. He was a year older, training with Bolton Wanderers, and on track to be a professional.

A flick of the ball, a dip of the shoulder, a spinning pass – The Twins were graceful players; they seemed to have more time than everyone else. And it wasn't just that. They were competitive, even aggressive, but stopped playing if someone was injured (or feigned injury) and congratulated team-mates and opposition alike on their play: 'Tekkers' and 'Skillage' and 'You're the best, man'. All of this would have been mocked if it had come from anyone apart from a brilliant player.

When the bell went, they walked off at the centre of a crowd of sporty kids, chatting and joking, kicking a ball around. Even Mark Roberts had fallen under their spell. The Twins said Mark was the best player on the pitch – which was nonsense, and Mark must have known it.

The sudden hand on my shoulder was Sam's. 'Hi, Ben! I was hoping you'd play.'

I was an OK footballer, but it would never have occurred to me to stand with the other guys when the teams were being picked. 'No, I don't usually play,' I said, looking down to the ground, surprised that he had remembered my name. 'Usually' was an overstatement; I had *never* taken part.

'Well, I want you on my team tomorrow,' Sam said. He raised his voice: 'Hey, guys, Ben's my first pick tomorrow!'

At that moment, I wanted to be like The Twins; I wanted to *be* them. Will suddenly seemed like a kid – these boys were like adults. I didn't consider the arrogance of it: Sam *knew* that he would be picking the teams the next day, despite the fact that he had just arrived at the school. That was simply the way it was going to be.

From behind, someone shouted, 'You don't want Bender on your team. He's shit.'

There was another voice: 'All he wants to do is mess around with that magic crap. How old is he? Ten?'

'I trust this guy,' Sam said, arm still casually draped around my shoulder, but turning to the voice. 'I reckon he's nearly as good as you. Tomorrow, Ben's my main man.' I felt muscles press against my back as he held me tighter.

You see? *I reckon he's nearly as good as you.* It wasn't quite an insult to the other kid, but could have been ironic, and it sounded like a compliment to me.

Something was shouted from a group of four boys who sat on a thick metal handrail in front of the classrooms. As usual, they'd ignored the bell, determined to slouch in last. These kids were even rougher than bullies like Darren, real thugs and druggies from the year below who didn't care about anything and would be leaving after one more year of doing nothing.

Jack strode over to them as if they were old mates. At first there were hand gestures and swearing from the four, but then Jack started talking and they straightened and laughed. I could hear, 'Yeah! Man!' and 'Yo! Dude!'

You see – it wasn't just me.

Will had been popular with girls in a general way, but I'd rarely spoken to any outside of lessons. There was one girl I sometimes talked to at chess club, but she was old-fashioned and a bit strange – people made fun of her. I had certainly never spoken to Caroline Termonde.

Caroline Termonde. I analysed every little look, searching for any glimmer of interest in me, but I was just background scenery in her A-level History class.

The History room was like being in a goldfish bowl: it had one big table in the middle and large windows that meant you could see people passing. Caroline came in and sat halfway down one side of the table, shaking her hair into place. I risked a tiny glance.

Behind Caroline, in the corridor, I saw Sam and Jack looking for the right room. They saw me and immediately shouted, 'Ben!' as if it were a fantastic surprise. I slapped hands with both of them and couldn't help looking at Caroline, just to make sure she noticed that I was in with the new kids.

'Hi – you must be Caroline,' Jack said as he sat down opposite her.

'Yeah,' she smiled. 'How d'you know my name?'

'You look like a Caroline.' Jack then turned his attention to me. 'Mate, it's good to see you.' And that killed the jealousy that had shot inside me.

Sam then sat next to his brother. 'Hi – you must be Ms Termonde.' He reached out his hand.

Caroline put two hands up and laughed. 'Come on, guys, how did you . . . ?'

'It's Ben – he mentally transmitted your name.' Sam waved his hands as if to show how the thoughts

14

had moved through the air.

Caroline turned to me. 'Hi, Ben.'

After four years, two words. She had said 'Ben'.

'Yeah – a bit of magic,' I said. My face was red but the words sounded OK.

Jack gestured to the pack that sat on top of my books. 'Got any tricks?'

I took a deep breath. The only person who'd ever spoken to me about tricks before was Blake. 'Yeah, OK.' I quickly 'shuffled' – that is, I organized the pack. Dr Richardson was bound to arrive any minute so I did a classic I'd practised a hundred times in front of the mirror at home.

It's dead easy: you ask someone to pick a card as you flick through the pack, but just hold back the last one with your index finger and let them see it for a fraction longer than the others. In this case, I held back the Queen of Hearts. Maybe that was a silly choice, but it's recognizable. Caroline fell for it – for such a simple trick, it's great that it never fails.

'Ben, that's really amazing, how did you do it?'

Nine more words!

'Magic?' I suggested.

'That's *so* wicked!' said Sam. 'Queen of Hearts!' And then in a whisper, 'Smooth.'

The handful of other kids who had come into the class muttered in appreciation and gave a patter of applause. One or two called me *Ben*.

Then Dr Richardson rushed in, sweaty and out of breath. The pile of books she was carrying spilt across the table and about ten fell on the floor. The Twins were down on their knees immediately, picking them up and asking if there was anything they could do to help.

I couldn't help looking at them as they responded to whoever was talking. When Dr Richardson spoke about Henry VII and the royal finances, they smiled and nodded with interest and understanding, or raised their eyebrows if surprised. When someone else was unsure, they frowned in sympathy. They seemed to give whoever was talking their complete attention.

After the lesson, we wandered along the corridor and I asked how they knew Caroline.

'Never seen her before,' said Sam.

'But you knew her name . . .' I started.

'Oh,' said Jack. 'We saw it.'

'On the Geography book poking out of her bag,' added Sam.

The conversation slid to magic. 'You're a natural,' Jack concluded. 'It must be in your blood.'

'I'm not sure what's in my blood,' I mumbled. Something made me rush to the truth. 'I might as well tell you . . . I don't know my dad.' I spoke so quietly that my lips hardly moved. 'My mother's dead. The only relation I have is my gran.' I shouldn't have been embarrassed.

Sam bent his right hand back so that I could see the inside of his wrist, then pointed at one of the veins with his left thumb. 'Look at that blood,' he said. 'It looks just the same as the blood pumping through you. You're no different to us.'

'I don't think I'm anything like you,' I said.

'You will be,' said Jack. 'Give it time. You will be.'

I only saw The Twins once more on that second day, in the Sports Hall as I headed to my after-school film club. There were about ten boys inside kicking a tennis ball around. I stood in the doorway, thinking that they were using the smaller ball to show off skills, but then saw that they were trying to kick the ball up so that it nestled behind one of the overhead lights – practically impossible. Jack's second attempt was weighted to perfection, but even that bobbled out, despite everyone cheering for it to stay.

'Come on!' said Sam as he bounced the ball from knee to knee before kicking up upwards. 'This is a

Challenge. You can't fail a Challenge.'

Soon after I walked away, I heard a huge cheer.

The Twins. The Challenge. You have to hear everything for a first time.

SEPTEMBER 2011
FIRST BLOOD

Apart from Will, no one from Wordsworth Academy lived in Compton Village, so I couldn't easily see friends after school. The Twins moved into a large house about four miles away, but it would only have been just over a mile away if Lake Hintersea hadn't been in the way. This chance nearness – I had no reason to think it was anything other than chance – was another reason I became close friends with them.

My only slight regret, as I became embedded near the centre of a large group of friends, was that Blake wasn't sure about them. He irritated me, but because of him I had never been entirely isolated.

'Come on, Blake,' I said on one occasion. 'Sam and Jack really want you to join us after school down the Rec.'

'Sam and Jack, Sam and Jack,' he echoed in a voice that was more nasally and nerdy than ever, 'Marcus and David, Marcus and David.'

I shook my head dismissively. 'What are you going on about? Marcus and David? I don't know anyone called

Marcus. David who? Has something snapped in your brain? Well, don't pretend I didn't offer,' I huffed. Much later, I learnt Blake was comparing Sam and Jack to human-looking robots from the *Terminator* films.

It was great to be able to talk about the Rec, a sort of tatty park, as if I were a veteran. It was where all the cool kids hung out after school, including lots of girls, though not Caroline. The Twins said their dad would take a detour through my village, the long way round Lake Hintersea, on the way back to their house, so I was able to go for the first time. It was Thursday of the second week of term, and we were there with Anna Whitney, Ethan Wingate and some others – all people who wouldn't have said a word to me a week before. We didn't do much to begin with, just played around the bandstand and jumped over the little stream. Just beyond the Rec was the river. The path and riverbanks were strewn with rubbish, and Ethan spotted two discarded supermarket trolleys.

'How did they get down here? The world's going to ruin, man.' Ethan played up to his reputation as a hippy. He was vegetarian and smoked weed from time to time.

'A Challenge,' said Sam.

'Do you want to ride, or do you want to drive?' Jack asked his brother.

It soon turned into races, one person riding in the trolley and another pushing.

After a couple of goes, Jack asked me if I wanted to be his driver.

'You bet,' I said. It was incredible that they'd had an effect so quickly. Jack was in one trolley, Sam in the other, and Anna volunteered to push him. That made the contest a fairly equal one, given that The Twins were identical in size and Anna and I had more or less the same strength.

Against the background of noise, Jack turned to me and whispered, 'Just go as fast as you can and as near to the edge as possible – see, the path's smoother there.'

'I don't want you to fall out.' I chuckled.

'I want it to be the fastest and best it can be,' Jack said. He looked me deep in the eyes, but I couldn't hold his gaze for long – it was as if The Twins looked right into my brain. 'Remember: I'm indestructible,' he muttered.

'Come on!' shouted Sam. 'If you've finished with the health and safety checks, it's first to the bench.'

Ethan stood to one side and lowered a tissue as if it were a flag in an American car race.

We raced along the path, The Twins urging us onward as if they were desperate jockeys. The bench was about 200 yards away, and it was a fast journey. The path was hardly wide enough for two, but we overtook them, they overtook us, and then we drew level as we passed the bench.

It was getting late after several races and a couple of people said that they had to get home.

'Just one more go,' said Sam. 'Jack and I'll take on anyone in a Challenge – a tenner says no one can beat us, even if they run and we have to push the trolley.'

It was surely a ridiculous bet, and Anna immediately took them up on it. She was one of the best athletes at school and even Usain Bolt couldn't have won if he had the disadvantage of pushing a trolley with someone in it. In fact, Anna did win – easily. But that's not the important thing.

Anna raced off – with no trolley to push, she was ahead from the start. The Twins' trolley rattled along very quickly, front wheels spinning and twisting, the carriage rocking from side to side. Jack was in the cart on his knees, leaning forward, his hands holding the metal at the front. Everyone else had sat in it like a baby in a pram, but Jack didn't see the danger – or maybe he just didn't care.

Sam leaned into the trolley and pushed with all his might. Neither Twin spoke.

It's hard to judge how fast, but they hurtled along the

path near to the edge at a speed that would have been reckless for a cyclist. Suddenly, the front right wheel hit a dip, the trolley stopped, buckled, and Jack was thrown out. Sam also fell, bruised by the trolley. But Jack was on the river side, and he went towards the drop – his hand grabbed for the trolley and then for the edge of the path, but not even he could overcome the power of gravity.

Sam was on his feet straight away, then disappeared over the edge to join his brother. Anna came back from the end of the path, took one look, and pressed three numbers on her mobile phone. We ran towards them.

I thought I'd see Jack bobbing around in the water, but he had fallen short and was in the muddy fringe immediately below the wall. Both of them were in the mud up to their knees, and it was difficult to tell which brother was which. But then I worked out that Sam was on the left, and they were both looking down at Jack's right leg.

'I'm fine,' said one.

'He's fine,' said the other.

Anna, who had a slightly different angle to me, continued with her call, asking for an ambulance *immediately*.

Moving along the path, looking at the imprints on the mud, and then seeing Jack, I saw what had happened: Jack had fallen on a piece of metal that had knifed through his upper leg about halfway between knee and hip.

The fifteen minutes before the ambulance came were surreal. The metal spike was poking out both sides of his leg, but Jack didn't cry, or scream or complain. He even limped along the muddy river edge to the point where he could get to the path, as if being speared was a minor inconvenience.

The ambulance crew didn't see it like that.

'Aren't you in pain, son?' one medic asked as he grimaced at the injury.

'Yes. I am,' said Jack calmly, his face expressionless.

'I think he's in shock,' whispered the medic.

'No,' said Jack, as if it were a ridiculous suggestion. 'I'm not in shock. I just want it dealt with and know my leg will bleed a lot if I just yank it out.'

We were interviewed by a couple of policemen, but it was clear from the crumpled trolley that the injury was the result of nothing more than a bunch of kids messing around.

I saw Jack sitting in the back of the ambulance, his brother leaning on the open rear door, when their dad arrived. He looked vaguely familiar, but I couldn't place him. Mentally logging him as The Twins' father meant that I didn't question it again.

'I'm sorry about this,' Jack said to him, shrugging with annoyance, then smiling at me as I appeared a few paces behind.

My gran would have had a nervous breakdown if she had seen me with a metal rod skewered through my leg, but Mr Thatcher didn't flinch: 'Has it gone through bone, or just muscle?' Those were his first words. Everything he said was practical.

'I think he's going to be fine,' said the paramedic in charge. 'Jack, how much does it hurt? Out of ten?' Perhaps he said this to get a more sympathetic tone from his father.

'Probably eight or nine,' said Jack. 'It's hard to measure because I've no comparison. It's a pain I've never felt before.'

'Well,' said another medic, 'you're being very brave. Let's get you to hospital and operate as soon as we can.'

'First, I need to speak to Ben,' Jack said, holding something in his hand. The paramedics tried to stop him, but Jack was insistent. 'I have to speak to Ben before we leave.'

I edged forward, struggling to draw my eyes away from the raised sheet that was draped over his leg.

'Here,' said Jack. 'Give this to Anna.' It was a crumpled

and slightly bloodstained ten-pound note.

I asked Jack afterwards how he managed to put up with so much pain. Did he feel pain less than other people? He said that he didn't know what others felt, but pain was just a feeling created in his brain that didn't actually *mean* anything; it was just something that you had to put up with.

'Pain's just a warning siren in your brain,' he said. 'You don't have to listen to it. It doesn't have to bother you.'

Jack spent the night in hospital and had to stay in the next day. Incredibly, against all medical advice, he returned to school on Monday using crutches, his leg bound up. He even hobbled around playing football at break.

Within two weeks, it was difficult to tell which twin was which again. I once saw a faint blood stain appear on Jack's trousers and asked him how long it would take for his leg to fully recover.

He said, 'It's annoying that we bleed, isn't it?'

SIX DAYS TO GO

📝 Draft Email

To:	
Cc:	
Subject: The Past	

Someone else has to know the whole truth.

'Christmas Eve, 2016. The middle of London, next to Big Ben. Midday,' he said. Then I watched him disappear into the woodland. With anyone else, they'd be empty words.

It was so far in the future I thought we'd never get here.

I came close to telling you everything when we went to Compton for Gran's funeral. You mentioned the view from the houses in Compton across Lake Hintersea and how it must be full of memories. 'Yeah,' I said. Just *Yeah – not I can remember what we did as if it was yesterday. Not I can remember the faces of those who died.*

Someone else |

SEPTEMBER 2011
SHADOW OF THE PAST

Compton Village was on a road that snaked between Lake Hintersea, one of the largest lakes in the Lake District, and Ward's Fell, one of the highest hills (we called it a mountain). It's on a hundred postcards. But in September 2011, Compton Village was still best known for a very rare thing: the mysterious death of a fifteen-year-old boy. 'Compton Village' was heard as 'Murdered Boy'. More than four months after the event, the police still hadn't found out what happened to Will.

One minute he was with me, circling in the road, and then he was gone – to be found two days later washed up on the shore of the Lake with a wound to the head. He had drowned.

His bike was left in the cemetery next to the church, and his boat was still tied up at the bottom of his garden. It was as if the Lake had grabbed hold of him while no one was looking – while *I* wasn't looking.

The newspapers were determined to get a van, driving slowly through the village, into the story. I hadn't seen one. Sailors on Lake Hintersea were interviewed; the police tracked down ramblers who walked down from Ward's Fell and past the churchyard; we were all spoken to several times. Nothing.

Locals believed he had been murdered. And they claimed to know who had done it. Mike Haconby was the fifty-something builder who lived in the house next to Will's, directly opposite me. His garden was overgrown, full of rubbish, a bicycle frame here, an old fridge there, a caravan rotting on his driveway. He had threatened us more times than we could remember in his slow, agitated voice.

'I'll *kill* you if you keep screeching and skidding your bikes in the lane'; 'I'll *kill* you if you don't keep quiet on the Lake'; 'If that ball comes into my garden, I'll destroy it and I'll *kill* you.'

He swore at us, which worried my gran in a way that his threats didn't. To be honest, Will wound him up on purpose.

For several days, forensic experts turned Mike's house upside down looking for a speck or fibre that would connect him to the murder, but found nothing. They dug up his garden. The panels of the old caravan were prised open. He didn't move away, though, despite the constant hounding and the whispered insults.

'Leave me alone. I've done nothing wrong – I don't want to leave Compton – it's my home,' Mike had said. His failure to move was seen as proof of his guilt. I'm sure that if he had moved, that would have been seen as equal proof.

Mike Haconby had discovered the body. He had been walking Bullseye along the shore of the Lake and just found Will there, among the lapping waves, just beyond the church, only a few steps from his bike. If you're the first to find the body, you're the last to see it alive – that's the logic. Guilty as charged, people said.

'He knew where to look.' Guilty as sin.

'Just look at that old caravan he has,' they said. 'I always knew he was weird.' Guilty. 'And all he does is walk around with that monster of a dog.'

But no one could explain how he did it. There's no way that Will would have gone with him without a fight. We all heard it a thousand times: *It was broad daylight; someone must have seen something.*

On the Saturday after Jack's accident I wanted to cycle to The Twins' house to see how he was, but was stopped before I left. 'Don't forget it's the last Saturday in the month,' my gran said from her chair in the front room.

I *had* forgotten. 'Gran, I'm on it.'

'And don't forget to speak nicely to everyone,' she added.

'Gran, I *have* done this before.' *A million times.*

'You're a good boy, Benny.'

For the last year, Gran had been more or less housebound, apart from church. She stayed in Compton Village, despite the remoteness, despite Will's death, even despite worries about me. I was also determined to stay. If anyone came to do the same to me as they did to Will, I would show them how much I hated them.

The village church (and its handful of old ladies) was the main thing in Gran's life, and delivering the monthly newsletters had been her job for forty years. Now, irritatingly, it had become mine.

I did all the houses on the eastern side of the Lake – eleven in total, of which seven were actually in the village. There was a twelfth house that I didn't deliver to: Will's. His parents had moved away 'temporarily' soon after his death. I suspected they moved because Mike Haconby hadn't.

It was crazy that Compton Village had a church. The village was only 300 yards from end to end with one much bigger house on the far side of the church: Lakeside House, where Mr and Mrs Winter lived. She was an artist and her husband was a recluse who, Gran said, was in a wheelchair. My mum worked there as a cleaner before I was born.

I usually saw no one as I cycled round, trying to get the job done in record time, but Mike Haconby was in his garden and it would have been awkward not to go straight to him.

'It's just the church newsletter,' I said.

Bullseye, his Leavitt Bulldog, barked and barked, always the same *bark-bark-bark* tune; even when I bravely put my upturned hand out to him, he aggressively danced around howling *bark-bark-bark*, closer and closer, until I lost my nerve and held my hand to my chest.

Mike was moving a large plant pot from one random location to another. His time would have been better spent tidying up the mess or mending the caravan. The innards of a broken lawnmower were sprawled across the lawn. Mike sniffed and scratched.

'Drop it on the mat,' he said slowly, as if he had to think about the words. Then he went back to dragging the pot.

'It's in here,' I said, prising open the letter box and trapping the newsletter so that it flapped in the breeze. I didn't want to drop it on the mat just because Mike had told me to. In any case, the wind would have blown it away. The door slowly creaked open. Copies of a tabloid newspaper were piled up next to a small table with a disconnected cream-coloured telephone; above that, there was an old painting of what looked like Lake Hintersea. With the door open fully, I saw his blue bag of tools. I remembered the same bag being taken out by the police when they were looking for a murder weapon. Bullseye jumped up, his paws leaving mud on my jeans. *Bark-bark-bark.*

Mike rubbed his lower back. 'Bullseye, down, down. Now!' He moved slowly.

My gran was probably the only person who thought he had nothing to do with Will's disappearance. 'I feel sorry for him,' she had said at the time. 'He can't even organize his garden. He doesn't mean any harm. He doesn't *mean* anything. He's a bit soft in the head.'

Now, delivering the newsletter, I tried to do what she said: 'Just be nice to him and keep your distance.'

'Benny,' he rasped in acknowledgement. 'I hope you're OK.'

'Yes. Fine,' I said blandly, and left as quickly as I came. Bullseye followed but never went further than the gate.

I don't need to tell you about all the houses I visited,

but one is of significance – Lakeside House. Like all the houses on the far side of the road, including Will's and Mike Haconby's, Lakeside House had direct access to the water. It was easily the grandest house in the area and had a large garden that stretched down to a wooden jetty.

I dreaded visiting Mike Haconby, but Lakeside House spooked me. Its driveway, overcast with trees, always seemed damp and cold, even at the height of summer. The house looked vaguely like a castle and had a stone tower, which we had always called the Lantern Room, at the top. It could be seen from miles away and at night was like a large, pale candle, poking up above the trees.

The house was significant because my mum worked there for fifteen years before I was born. I couldn't imagine the smiling woman in the photo on my gran's sideboard walking up and down the dreary lane.

At the bottom of its long garden was a rowing boat that Will and I went out in when we were little. Mrs Winter was happy that we used it, and Will's parents and my gran didn't ask what we were up to. One day when I was ten, I fell overboard, gulped in water rather than air, and in my confusion rose underneath the boat. I still shudder at the fizzing, swirling water and my panic and disorientation. My blood runs cold at the thought that Will experienced the same thing before he died. But Will dived in and rescued me. Without him, I would have died.

Since then, I'd not been on Lake Hintersea once. The rowing boat bobbed about on the jetty, unused.

In my whole life, even though he lived a few hundred yards away, I'd only seen Mr Winter once – as I lay on his lawn waiting for the ambulance to come on the day I almost drowned. He only said one thing: 'I've watched you; you're a good boy.'

Mrs Winter (I always called her that, never Daphne) usually worked in a conservatory studio on the Lake Hintersea side of the house, and was friendly, loud and eccentric, the exact opposite to her husband. Every other word was 'darling' or '*daaahling*'.

She appeared down the side of the house as I was about to get back on my bike. 'Thank you, my darling,' she started. 'Thank you so very much.'

'No problem,' I replied.

'And, darling, how are you now? Are you feeling better?'

The second question was easier to answer. 'Yes, thank you.' I hoped that short responses would speed my escape.

'You know, darling, that the Lake is out there waiting for you. Your mother would have liked you to be out there.' She smiled, her thin lips overlaid with heavy red make-up.

Green eyes. 'It's a shame that the boats are unused.'

Will had used a Topper, a small craft designed for one, which was still at the bottom of his back garden. He would often be on the Lake without me, sometimes with his dad, usually on his own.

'No, thank you. Sailing isn't my thing,' I said, my head filled with a vision of Will cutting through the water on his boat, then reminded of the nightmare of bubbles and confusion that had haunted me since my own accident, and doubly since Will's death.

'Well, the offer stands for as long as those hills,' she continued, smiling, apparently oblivious to my discomfort. 'It's so good to see you around, *darling*, so very good.'

A shadow moved behind a net curtain in the window high above her.

The rowing boat bobbed on the jetty.

'Thank you, Mrs Winter,' I said.

She had been kind to us, supplying ice lollies when we returned from the Lake, even, once, letting us dab at one of her paintings. It was a very modern creation, barely resembling the Lake at all, and I remembered Will joking afterwards that a three-year-old could have done it and it wouldn't have mattered where he left his splodge.

Happy days. Lucky days.

*

But as I rode back down the driveway to Lakeside House, another memory returned.

There was only one time I had a serious argument with Will: Good Friday, 2011, about two weeks before he drowned.

In the school holidays, we would spend every afternoon together, often whole days. We usually met at 2.30. 'It's half past two, Will will be waiting,' my gran would say, and sometimes just 'Will-will', as if it was some sort of animal call.

In those Easter holidays, Will missed some of our meetings. 'It's not a date in my diary,' he said. 'We've never actually arranged it.'

But for me, 2.30 p.m. meant 'Time to see Will'.

Many times I'd wait at the bottom of his garden while Will raced back in his small boat, waving and shouting, as I looked warily at the water. But that final Easter – the warmest Easter on record and with hardly any rain – Will often went out without telling me, and sometimes he didn't return all afternoon.

About two weeks before he died, I went over the road to see Will as usual and his mum said that he was sailing on Hintersea.

'Didn't he tell you?' she asked. 'I haven't known you two have a falling out before.' She smiled sympathetically.

It was the thought that I had done something to upset Will that kept me at the bottom of his garden all afternoon. It was a hot day, much more like July than April – exactly the sort of day that should produce happy memories. I just stared out at the Lake, getting more and more upset, my neck turning pink, then red.

Later than he'd promised his mum he'd return, Will gradually became more defined as he edged out of the haze.

'I've been waiting here for hours!' I shouted as soon as he was within earshot. I was all emotion – common sense completely burned away. 'I've been waiting here for bloody hours!'

Will landed the boat on the small shoreline, splashed out, and tied it to the usual post without looking at me.

Selfish, sad tears were welling up in my eyes. 'I can't believe that you're not even talking to me now, when I've been waiting for you for hours.'

Will spat out his words. 'I was *only* out on the Lake; you *know* I like to go out on the Lake; I didn't ask you to *wait*; we're not *married*.' He tutted and swore. 'Well, if I'm your *slave*, what would you like me to do now?'

He stood with his hands in the pockets of his blue shorts – the shorts he was wearing when he died. I was no longer sure whether I was in the right or the wrong, and that kept me going, shouting about how unfair he was.

We had never come close to blows before, but he hit me – a slap, right hand against my left cheek, hard enough to leave a light red smudge.

'That's to bring you to your stupid senses,' Will shouted, eyes aflame. 'There are some things that we have to do on our own. I'm not jealous of your magic tricks.'

The mention of jealousy touched a nerve. I stormed off, shoulders heaving up and down as I cried. I lowered my head as I saw Mike Haconby silently watching from his garden, then put my hands over my face as I passed Will's mum.

About mid-evening, Will rang our front door bell instead of shouting at my window. He started by saying that his mum had told him to apologize.

'Well, I'm sorry, too,' I said. I had cried out my frustration, and my apology and red eyes probably encouraged Will to make genuine amends.

'Sorry, mate,' he said with sincerity. 'I'll try not to do it again.'

'Is it something I've done? I just wanted us to go

out on our bikes as we used to.'

'I suppose things change as you get older,' Will said.

I returned home from delivering the newsletters at exactly the same time that a Royal Mail van stopped in the lane.

The postman handed me four letters from his pile and said I could save his legs. I flicked through the delivery. Under an advert for a stairlift and something from a charity, above what I supposed was a bill, there was a smaller letter for me. Above my address it said: *Benny (Private)*. No surname.

I never received letters – no one from school would use such an old-fashioned way of communicating unless they were forced to.

'Junk mail on the table,' I shouted, then turned back out the door, opening the envelope as I went. Inside was a small white piece of card.

It started: *Hi Benny*

At the end I could see: *Will (Capling)* – just like that, with the surname in brackets.

I stood still and read the name over and over: *Will (Capling)*, *Will (Capling)*, *Will (Capling)* . . . My insides churned.

I immediately thought it was a sick joke, and probably

would have torn it up or run inside and moaned about it to my gran, had it not been for the handwriting, which looked like Will's – and one line towards the end:

Think of me whenever you eat a curliewurly.

This wasn't the chance line of a random 'joker'; it was an embarrassing joke that I'm certain only Will and I shared – for us, 'a curliewurly' didn't mean the chocolate bar. There was surely no way that such a thing would be known by someone casually impersonating Will.

There was no doubt that Will was dead. Absolutely no doubt: there had been forensic experts, an autopsy, funeral people, and a burial. People had seen his dead body.

Hi Benny. I'M NOT DEAD.

Everyone wants to know what happened to me - I know that.

Look, I know I can trust you. Its important you dont tell anyone at all. Definately not the police.

PLEASE just play along. Perhaps you'll want to tell Sylvie or my parents, but don't.

(Think of me whenever you eat a curliewurly. I'll be back.)

Will

The postmark said *Manchester*.

I went back inside and up to my room, knelt on the

41

floor and put the letter on the bed. Who would want to play such an awful joke? Darren Foss had bullied me badly, verbally and physically, but I didn't think this was his style. But maybe it was.

'Sylvie' was what Will called my gran, but anyone could have known that.

I leaped across the room and pulled down a box from the top shelf of my wardrobe. This was 'Will's Box', a collection of memories we assembled after Will died – it was meant to help me get over the shock and remember Will in a calm, positive way. There were all sorts of odds and ends, everything from a poster of our favourite film to a little plastic Smurf. It included Will's Rough Book from school – I think I got it because everyone knew only I would understand most of the scribbles inside. After I put it on the bed, I flicked through the bottom right-hand corner and a little stick-man waved his arms and legs in the air. The last few stick-men pictures also had something else rudely waving around. Typical.

On the first page inside he had drawn two cartoon characters: him (strong, girls in the background, a six-pack); and me (weedy, massive Y-fronts, red spots). The title: *this is Me and you.*

Everyone wants to know what happened to Me . . . this is

Me and you: 'Me', not 'me', in the middle of a sentence. Will was creative, but not good at anything that involved accuracy, like spelling and grammar.

At the bottom of the same page, next to a rude and amusing illustration, I also saw '*curliewurly*'.

Not Curlywurly: 'curl*ie*wurly', with only one *y*.

I closed the book and threw it back in the box. Even the cover, splattered with little drawings and comments, made me sad.

The note was either a chillingly good hoax, or somehow, God only knew how, Will had written it.

Written it? Posted it? No way. It was much, much easier to think it was a cruel joke.

I stood in the window to see if a sicko (Darren?) was watching and laughing. Nothing. Nothing apart from Mike Haconby walking up his garden path. Bullseye barked loudly.

It was only then that I turned the card over and saw someone had drawn the most basic unhappy face – dots for eyes and nose, an upturned half-circle for a mouth, all inside a circle. It was exactly the sort of thing that Will would have done.

I didn't want to believe it was genuine, but put it away with Will's things in the box.

There was an irritated shout from the bottom of the stairs.

'I wish you wouldn't leave your bike in the middle of the path all of the time.'

'I'm just leaving to see The Twins,' I called back, trying to sound normal, but feeling tearful.

'Daphne Winter will be round this afternoon for an hour,' my gran said, again mentioning a major event for her. 'Tea at six. I'm doing eggs and chips.'

'OK.' I buried my head in my duvet and cried.

I *should* have gone downstairs and talked about the card. My gran was in her mid-seventies but she was still sharp when it came to anything involving common sense. I *could* have taken it to the police, but that would have dredged up the horror of what happened before. It would put me back in the shadow just as I was beginning to escape from it. Once the moment passed, the note seemed crazy and unreal, a little shard from a nightmare that had pierced into real life.

I think crying helped push emotion out of me. *Whoever has sent this – I'm not going to give them the satisfaction of getting to me.*

I rode off, jittery and unsettled, oversensitive to a world

that, for a time, had brighter colours and louder sounds. *How could anyone be such a bastard to have sent me a card like that?*

A few hundred yards down the lane, everything seemed calmer again, and I tried to force thought of the letter into a corner of my brain. But every part of that journey made me think of Will.

At the head of the Lake, between the trees, at a point where sunlight burst through the shadows, I saw Cormorant Holm, the island in the middle of Lake Hintersea. Beyond it, the Winters' rowing boat bobbed about on their jetty.

SEPTEMBER 2011
STAIRWAY TO HEAVEN

On the opposite side of the Lake to Compton Village there was another hill, not quite as high as Ward's Fell. The bottom third of the slope was thick with trees, and among them there was Timberline, where The Twins lived.

It took me about twenty minutes, that Saturday after Jack's injury, and still reeling from Will's letter, to cycle to the bottom of the twins' drive, and then nearly another ten to climb up the track that zigzagged through the trees. It was steep enough for me to get off my bike and push. The road curled round, and on a ledge, above a sixty-foot sheer drop, was Timberline. The house wasn't huge in the way that Lakeside House was, but it was impressively built in dark yellow stone and covered in ivy and other greenery. People who went to Wordsworth Academy didn't usually have fancy houses. A Land Rover was on a gravel drive between the house and the drop.

I glanced into a room with bookshelves and then one with a large dining-room table. Gravel crunched.

'Bloody hell,' I muttered, impressed. Then I looked to

46

my right, across Lake Hintersea towards Compton Village and Ward's Fell. I could see the turret at the top of Lakeside House.

My mind went back to the letter yet again. I wondered about mentioning it at school and getting the writer expelled – I imagined that being Darren Foss.

The front door had a fish-shaped brass knocker, but before I had a chance to use it, Sam opened it.

'Your parents must be loaded!' I said, a little too loud.

'We don't feel rich,' Sam shrugged. 'We're just ordinary kids.' He smiled. Typical of The Twins – not really telling me anything. 'The invalid is upstairs . . .'

The house looked the way that cool rich people's houses do. There was modern art on most of the walls and no carpet on the floor, just smooth wooden boards. On the right, just before the stairs, I caught a glimpse of a large harp in the sitting room.

'Can you play?' I asked.

'Just a little bit,' Sam said as he wandered in and ran his fingers up the strings. He then played about ten seconds of a Led Zeppelin song.

'I think that's the biggest painting I've ever seen,' I said, pointing at what was hanging behind him – it must have been twelve feet by six, a swirly sky above a mountain, crooked houses at the bottom. It was vaguely Van Gogh in style, I suppose.

Jack's bedroom had posters and photos behind perspex frames (not a bit of Blu-tack in sight) – one was a signed photo of a famous football manager with the message: *To Jack – when the time comes, wear red for me.* There was also a banner poster running at the top of the wall behind his bed: THE CHALLENGE.

Jack was sitting in bed with a computer keyboard on his lap and two screens on a desk in front of him.

'Hey, Ben, my man,' he shouted and raised a hand for me to slap. 'They said that if it had gone through the bone I would have been in plaster for three months.' His leg was heavily bound and raised on a cushion. 'Give it a couple of days and I'll be back in action.'

'Imagine if it had been a bit higher and to the left: the pole would have disappeared up his arse!' Sam laughed. 'He's being a lazy git. I wanted to abseil down the cliff earlier and he just sat there like a blob.'

I wasn't sure whether Sam was joking about the abseiling.

Jack told me about the short but grisly operation to remove the pole. He could have been kept in hospital for longer, but there was no infection and everything was predicted to heal well if he rested.

'And it means that I can sit here setting some wicked Challenges.' It was that word again.

'Challenges?' I asked.

'Oh, it's just a game,' he said airily.

Again, I thought about the note from 'Will' and zoned out.

'Is everything OK, Ben?' said Jack, putting the keyboard to one side.

Hi Benny. I'M NOT DEAD.

Everyone wants to know what happened to Me - I know that.

Look, I know I can trust you. Its important you dont tell

anyone at all.

'Ben,' said Sam, 'if something's up, we want to be in on it.'

Since Will died, secrecy was natural for me, but The Twins managed to drag out a half-truth. 'I was just thinking about a friend of mine who died,' I said. 'It was four months ago, but . . .' This was the moment to tell them, but I let it slip away. 'Sometimes things happen that make me think about him.'

'We heard,' said Jack with concern and a hint that he felt awkward talking about something that upset me. 'Is it right that he was killed?'

I felt exposed when the Twins looked straight at me: their dark brown eyes seemed so bright, as if little lasers were being fired.

'Yes. An *unsolved* murder,' I said. 'Or almost certainly a murder. I was there seconds before he was taken. I was the last person to see him,' I mumbled. 'Apart from whoever did it.'

'Let's hope we find out who it was,' said Sam. 'Then we can get him – and make him *pay*.'

'Or her,' said Jack. 'Whoever it is, we'll smash them.'

We had become allies. But they didn't press for more information – instead, Sam leaped up and pointed at me with both index fingers.

'I've got it,' he said, face alight with an idea, 'if Jack is going to lie there like a beached whale, you can come abseiling with me. We've got all the kit. And we've got . . . the cliff.'

With Jack lucky not to have been speared up the backside, I was worried (as well as fascinated) by what the The Twins' daredevil natures would lead to next.

'I'm not so sure,' I said evasively. 'I've never done that before. I wouldn't really . . .'

'We've done it a *thousand* times. We've abseiled down and we've climbed up. We call it the "Stairway to Heaven".

If you like, you can feed the safety line. You don't have to go down if you don't want to.'

The ropes had to be threaded through something at the top of the cliff, and the solution was clever: Sam leaped in the Land Rover and, spinning the steering wheel with one hand, swung it round until the back was about five feet from the cliff. Ropes were threaded through hooks above and below the back door.

'I'm not so sure about this,' I said nervously. 'I don't want to get the blame if something goes wrong.' This was the old Benny talking.

Jack had hobbled next to me at the top of the cliff. 'I couldn't stay away,' he said. 'Maybe I can help you with the safety rope?'

Sam put on a Black Diamond helmet that weighed about as much as a baseball cap, and went down twice. With the safety rope being fed through the Land Rover's hooks and a metal clasp, there wasn't much that could actually go wrong.

The Twins didn't pester me to have a go. They didn't even encourage or hint – just slowly drew me into their world. 'You're miles better with that safety rope than Jack,' said Sam.

'I think I want a go,' the new Ben blurted.

A harness came out of the large black equipment bag, then a clasp, then Sam handed me his helmet – and with each piece of kit I retreated to being nervous.

'You can say no at any time,' Jack reassured me as he checked my harness. 'We're not setting you a Challenge.'

I wiggled my head to make sure that the helmet was tight. I was going to do it; I didn't want to let them down.

'I'll go on the safety rope for Ben,' said Sam.

'I'm fine with it, really,' said Jack.

It was the first time I'd seen them disagree. Then: 'We'll both . . .' they said together. Perfect, as always.

Standing at the top, looking over my shoulder down three miles of Lake Hintersea, all of the setting of my life was within sight. Cormorant Holm was between Timberline and Compton Village. I thought of Will in his boat. Somewhere out there behind me was the answer . . .

I let myself down one step, then two, and lost sight of Timberline behind the rock face. If anything went wrong now, there would be nothing to stop sixty feet of gravity's pull. My legs weakened, but then grew stronger with each small step, and the steps gradually became more like jumps.

'OK down there?' shouted one of The Twins.

About halfway down, my feet dislodged looser rock and sent it spilling down, bouncing off the cliff wall as it went, and then I came to a halt. I tried to jump down as I had before, but swung back against the same part of the cliff. The rope wasn't being fed through.

'Guys, what's going on up there?' I shouted.

No response.

'Guys? I hope you're not arsing about!'

Nothing.

I started to fall.

It's a horrible feeling, of course, when you start falling and feel that all of your insides are a few seconds behind the rest of you. I made a sort of yawning noise as I breathed in heavily. Immediate panic. My hands and feet waved about pathetically.

But I fell only three feet before I came to a sudden jolting stop, the wind taken out of me. 'What the hell?' I shouted.

A face appeared over the edge about forty feet above me. 'Don't worry – it's just the rope, but we've sorted it now, mate – bounce off just as you did before . . .'

I gingerly continued on my way. Gradually the ground came closer and closer until I could shout that I had reached the bottom. YES!

'What was all that about?' I said, when I reached the top.

'It's the rope,' said Jack. 'Sometimes a knotty bit gets caught in the hook.'

I looked at the rope. Some of it was a little uneven, perhaps. Sam said that he would go down once more to try to prove that he was still better than me.

'I challenge you do it in two leaps,' said Jack.

'Challenge?' said Sam.

'Yes, a Challenge,' Jack said. 'If you make it, I'll slave for you for the rest of the day – even with this leg.'

'Piece of piss,' responded Sam. 'You're on!' As they slapped hands, Sam turned to me: 'My brother sometimes underestimates what we can do.'

What *we* can do.

'I'll be on the safety rope,' I offered.

I offered Sam the helmet but he shook his head, flicked his hair back, quickly threaded one rope through a harness, and disappeared over the edge without any safety back-up. I was so surprised by his athleticism and bravery (or madness?). It was like watching a superhero.

I raced to the edge to see Sam swing against the side, already twenty-five feet down, in complete control. He shouted 'Yeah!' and then, letting the rope escape through his fingers at just the right speed, without any further bounces against the cliff, reached the bottom with the grace of an experienced abseiler. Incredible.

'Does that count as two leaps or one?' he shouted as he threaded the spare rope through his harness. Straight away, he started sprinting up the zigzag driveway.

'I'm going to do it in one leap,' Jack said, looking over the edge. 'But only when I can, and that will be when Sam Challenges me.'

'See?' Sam panted as he returned. 'You don't really need the safety rope. But we're all human, aren't we, Jacko?' He playfully patted Jack's leg.

I then went down a second time, faster, better. There were no problems with the rope. I had nothing to fear with The Twins around.

'You're sick at this,' said Sam. 'We should have Challenged you.'

'What's with these Challenges?' I asked, looking between house, Twins, and the magnificent view of the Lake towards Compton Village, knowing that my life was changing. 'Is it your game?'

Sam draped his arm around his brother's shoulder. '*Our* game? S'pose it's a game,' he said. 'And sometimes more than a game.'

They looked out across the Lake and laughed.

OCTOBER 2011
MAGIC

It was on the last Friday of the October half-term that The Twins held a Halloween party at their house. The email read: *The Thatcher Twins invite you to a Halloween and Firework Party. We want to thank you for welcoming us to the Lakes.* Parties like this didn't happen often in our part of the world.

I glanced at myself for a fifth time in the mirror. There wasn't much in my wardrobe, but I eventually decided on a dark blue hoodie with a logo plastered across the front – the most expensive piece of clothing I owned. It reminded me of the hoodie Will used to wear. My 'costume' was the standard Scream mask.

Ethan had offered to give me a lift to the party.

'Hey, man,' he had drawled the day before, 'we need to, like, share the world's resources.' I didn't mention the environmental impact of his father's Jaguar XF – but my gran hardly drove her car any more, and I hadn't started driving lessons yet, so relied on others.

The short journey from my house to Timberline was

filled with Ethan's father rattling off questions with a fluency that suggested he'd asked them before. I sat silently in the back next to Anna, looking anywhere but at her.

'How many people will be there?' was one question.

'I dunno,' said Ethan, his voice lower and lazier than ever. 'Like, loads. Definitely tens. Maybe hundreds.' He turned round to me and mouthed: *Millions?*

His father immediately took a different tack. 'And who will be in charge? Who will make sure nothing goes wrong?'

Yawning and stretching drew out Ethan's responses. 'Like, loads of grown-ups, really responsible people, The Twins' parents, geezers like that.'

'Sorry about my old man,' said Ethan as we walked up the zigzag lane to The Twins' house. 'He was never young.'

Ethan had suggested it would be nice but dull, with people sitting around like monks, but the reality was totally different. There were signs of adult involvement – food, signs for the toilet, organized drinks – but I never saw anyone older than us from the beginning to the end of the evening. That, and the remoteness of the location, generated a buzz.

Sam and Jack were standing near the door as we

approached, each with a bottle of beer in hand. Music pumped from somewhere near, and there was the raucous chatter that suggested a lot of people had already arrived. The cliff I had abseiled down a couple of weeks before was in darkness off to the right.

'Hey, it's the great Ben,' said Jack. 'The action man.'

I was flattered that they had mentioned me first, but we had been spending a lot of time together in school as well as outside.

'And the dude Ethan; and a girl I really want to hug,' added Sam as he stepped forward.

Anna's witch's hat fell off as she held on to Sam for slightly longer than seemed necessary.

Some people had been serious about their costumes (zombies, skeletons, witches) but others hadn't dressed up at all. Most, including The Twins, had done next to nothing – Sam's and Jack's nods to the theme were their T-shirts: they had cartoon representations of themselves (and doing what they could, as always, to help everyone distinguish them). One was drawn in orange pyjamas, face half hidden by a sack with buttons for eyes, with '*Samhain*' written underneath; the other had a pumpkin-like head with a candle-like body above '*Jack-o'-Lantern*'. Original.

More people were arriving behind us and Anna and Ethan were moving away.

'Ben, we'll see you around,' said Sam. 'Don't neglect us.'

'Yeah, OK,' I said, slightly uneasy with such a big party. 'Sure.'

Jack put his arm around me and whispered conspiratorially. 'We really *will* see you around,' he said. 'I know we've invited all these people, but you're different.' I felt his breath on my ear.

Only some of the party took place in the house, and most of that was in a large conservatory at the far end. There was a double garage open and a summer house in the trees beyond that, the path lit by lights on a string.

I had wandered over to the garage where there was a vast supply of alcohol – three tables were stocked with beer cans and bottles (there were already quite a few gaps), and another had wine and spirits.

A lot of people were smoking in the summer house, and not all were smoking ordinary cigarettes. Ethan inhaled deeply and offered me something from a clear plastic pouch pulled from his inside jacket pocket. Fear of the unknown, and stories of how people die after a bad experience with drugs, made me hesitate.

'No thanks, mate,' I said. 'I should see if Blake's here.'

I went back to the gravel drive in front of the main house just in time to see Blake arriving with his parents. The invite email had been clear: *Drop-off and collection at the bottom of the track, please.* It didn't quite say *You're doing A-levels now, don't bring Mummy and Daddy*, but everyone else got it. What's more, if Blake's parents either saw the drink, or anything that hinted of drugs, Blake would be dragged away and the police called.

I was about to run over, but Sam was there before me, an orange and black jacket hiding his T-shirt. I could just about hear him. 'Mr and Mrs Caudwell, isn't it? Have you come to join us?'

Blake's parents were nice people who lived in the 1950s. 'We just wanted to be sure Blake got here safely,' his mother said frostily, determined to be shocked.

'Our parents usually come down when it's time to eat; they'd be delighted to meet you if you want a cup of tea,' Sam said.

I still wonder if it was a lie. In any case, we didn't see The Twins' parents at any point that evening. And if it *was* a lie, and his parents *weren't* there, it was a massively risky one.

'Oh, no, but thank you awfully,' Blake's dad said,

pulling his tie knot a little to let in some air after the steep climb. 'We wouldn't want to intrude, would we, dear?' He looked up at the house, (probably) impressed and (almost certainly) intimidated in the same way I had been.

The mention of 'parents' and 'tea' had visibly softened Mrs Caudwell. 'A very nice offer. We'll see you at eleven o'clock sharp at the bottom of the drive,' she instructed Blake.

Sam then extended his hand to shake Mr Caudwell's, which meant moving a can of Sprite from right to left. Mrs Caudwell actually forced out a thin smile at his politeness.

Blake was only there because I had pestered him, and from the start seemed only a breath away from saying how much he hated it. But he couldn't stop his quirky character amusing us.

After half an hour with Blake, Anna (who seemed to think Blake was a circus act), an increasingly spaced-out Ethan and I went back to the garage to collect beers. Caroline Termonde was there, shoulder to shoulder with Mark Roberts. He had been nice to me in the Summer term after Will died; everyone had said he was the right choice as Wordsworth Academy's Head Boy. Seeing him with Caroline, I felt that fiery mix of irrational hatred and frustration that is jealousy. He was, I suddenly decided, bland and smarmy, more of a weak teacher than a great pupil. Of all the boys in the school for Caroline to go for, he was one of the worst choices.

'OK there, Ben?' said Mark.

OK there, Ben? There? What did that mean? I hated his blond curly hair and oh-so-trendy glasses worn instead of contact lenses. How could Caroline go for such a piece of cardboard?

'Yeah, great. Good to see you,' I replied, suddenly sure I was in the same league as the likes of Mark. I was the one who had been to The Twins' house already; I was the one who had abseiled down the cliff.

'Hi, Ben! You're in my History class,' said Caroline as she put her arms loosely around my shoulders in the way girls do when they don't really want to touch you.

'Just getting some beers; see you around,' I said, but they weren't really listening.

Things went from bad to worse. Blake came round the corner from the garden, probably looking for me – and at exactly the same time, Darren Foss strode across the gravel with the two thugs who were in the toilets when I first met The Twins. Darren had been less obnoxious since, but even The Twins' impact seemed to be fading. None of us had understood the iron resolve of The Twins.

'What you doing here?' said Darren, heading straight for Blake. 'You don't come to this sort of thing.' Darren had already been drinking.

Blake looked at me and then at the sky. His first *I told you so*. At first, I thought he was going to stand his ground, but then he made an ungainly scamper into the woods beyond the garage. He should have known better.

Whooping, Darren and his friends dashed after him. 'Let's get Blakey!' they shouted. 'Hunt the piggy! Make him squeal!'

Swearing in frustration, I followed. Out of the corner of my eye I saw Mark Roberts do the same. I didn't think it was any business of his and, football star or not, there was no way I would let him overtake me.

I saw Darren point for one of his friends to go left and right to hunt Blake down. I thought they wouldn't hurt him badly, not with so many people around, but it wouldn't have been surprising if Blake reappeared without his trousers, or worse. Sound and light from the party leaked into the woods to begin with, but soon faded away.

After about thirty paces, with Mark's thudding footsteps behind me, just as it was getting too dark to distinguish trees from the black of night, I saw the white stripes of Darren's top. Blake had stopped before a small ravine and its hidden, gurgling stream.

'Come on, Blakey,' I heard Darren say in the near distance. 'We just want to have a laugh. It's only a joke.'

For a dreadful moment, I thought Blake was going to jump. He turned and looked at the drop a couple of times.

'If you lay a hand on me,' he said in his usual nasally tones, 'I'll go straight to the police . . . and Mr Morris.' Mr Morris was our no-nonsense Headmaster – this was an appeal to authority Blake had made many times before.

'Don't be such a tosser,' Darren said. Then much louder: 'Guys, I've found him.'

The only nearby sound was the cracking of twigs as Mark and I edged closer.

Darren shouted again: 'Guys, I'm over here. Guys?' I saw the pale circle of Darren's face as he turned around.

'Leave him alone,' I said. It was the first time I'd properly stood up to Darren.

'Benny? Yeah? Yeah?' His hands were already fists. 'And what are *you* going to do about it?' His laugh came out as a giggle. 'Your *new* best friends aren't here to help you now.'

'Just come back to the party, Darren.' It was Mark's low voice.

After years of practice, Darren knew how to be slippery,

and he immediately adjusted to Mark's arrival.

'That's what I'm trying to do, but Blakey legged it like a complete knob. What's wrong with trying to help someone? Don't start picking on me just because you're Head Boy. You're not Head Boy here.' Darren swore as he tripped over a root and caught a branch under his chin. 'You should stay away from me,' he called over his shoulder a few seconds later. 'I want to know what you're up to in this forest anyway, Benny. Looking for something? I've heard about people like you.' And he walked back towards the house.

It wasn't easy to get Blake to return to the party, but I reluctantly accepted it would have been impossible without Mark's intervention.

'Aren't you guys into magic?' Mark asked patronizingly – as if the gap between us was years rather than months. 'Blake, why don't you come in and see Ben do some tricks? Maybe you can do one yourself?'

Blake initially insisted that he should ring home – 'That's what I've been told to do if there's any trouble' – but the promise of magic finally deterred him, though not without many hints of *I told you so*. I was keen to do some tricks because Mark would bring Caroline, and she would be impressed by what had happened, given that I was the first to run after Darren, and Mark had actually run after me, which wasn't nearly as brave.

We returned to find Darren surrounded. 'We went off into the woods to try to help this idiot,' he said, pointing at Blake, 'and now Chrisso and Chalkie have disappeared.' I hoped that his caveman friends had fallen into a ditch.

'Would you like us to look again?' asked Jack. 'They might have gone further than we thought.'

A bizarre quarter of an hour followed, during which members of the party drunkenly wandered in and out of the woods with the pretence of looking for the lost pair. Couples went off together and sometimes took suspiciously long to return.

Ethan shrugged and turned back to the house, but I also went looking, using the torch on my phone. It was hard to judge distances, but I went further than anyone else, higher up the slope, and found a track that had been driven on, presumably by the Land Rover. I later discovered that my theory was right: a track snaked behind the house and out into the forest, through the trees to the right of Timberline if you were looking across the river from Compton Village.

I went far beyond where it was likely Darren's friends had wandered. The sound of the party didn't reach this part of the woods. After three or four bends in the track, I knew I was being stupid, but in the distant gloom I could see a splitting of the tracks. I shone the torch behind me (nothing), then pushed the beam into my leg for a second (total black in all directions).

I don't know why I went so far – perhaps I subconsciously knew that there was something to be found? To the right, off the main track, there was a large shed, the size of a double garage. A chain and padlock were wound tightly round the handles.

Almost immediately, I heard something approaching behind me, fast. My head instinctively turned into the darkness, and by the time the torch pointed in the right direction I caught the blur of a Twin approaching. For a moment I thought he was going to rugby tackle me, and I flinched, but he slid to a stop.

'Ben, have you got lost?'

'No, I was just looking, and the track kept on going, and . . .' I felt like a complete idiot.

'Let's get back,' said Sam. 'Let's see if those two morons have been found.'

The wooden building slipped back into darkness and silence.

*

My phone's torch dimly lit the track for both of us. We wandered back to the others, talking about the area and how much we liked it. I explained about my phobia of water, and how strange it was that I had lived the past six years next to millions and millions of gallons of something that frightened me.

'How did you come to move here?' I asked.

'Timberline has been in the family for some time,' said Sam. 'But we're now here permanently.'

'So you know the area?'

'Yeah – a bit.'

He didn't actually *lie*.

'Actually, I wondered if I recognized your father,' I said.

'Maybe in a car going through Compton? Though we usually drive in the other way,' Sam suggested. From the main road at the top of the Lake, it would be quicker to go down the right-hand side of Lake Hintersea, rather than through Compton Village.

In a car? *No*, I thought, *that's not it*. But I couldn't work out where . . . *I had seen his face before. Close up, maybe on television* . . .

I wondered about their previous school – they had hardly spoken about anything to do with their past. It slipped out in one lesson that they understood Latin, which wasn't taught anywhere I knew. 'Which school were you at in London?' I asked.

The noise of the party was slowly returning.

'I don't mind you knowing *anything* – but don't want anyone else to know.' Sam smiled and nodded as if this was a significant fact. 'We were at a boarding school just outside London,' he murmured. 'But we definitely prefer Wordsworth.' I didn't care that they had been somewhere posh. I didn't ask why they had moved, and I didn't ask any more questions. They had never mentioned old friends or anything about their life before Wordsworth.

Almost as soon as we returned, Darren's accomplices stumbled out of the woods, first the ratty one, then the ape. Everyone gathered to look. Both appeared to have run into trees or ditches, but they claimed to have been attacked. One had a bruise on his shoulder; the other was bleeding.

'One of you little turds was playing with us, man!' said the smaller one. 'When I find out who, I'll smash your skull!' ape-man threatened to no one in particular.

I know what you're thinking. The Twins somehow did it. I still don't see how they could have. There was so little time. They would have had to find them and beat them up, all without being noticed – even by their victims – who weren't together at the time. But if anyone could have done it, it was Sam and Jack. In any case, someone, or something, did.

'You're a couple of thick and clumsy idiots,' said Mark.

'I didn't . . . Someone . . . in the darkness . . .' rat-face started.

'He had a stick . . .' said ape, sensing that his story was doubted. He turned to Darren for support. 'I've had enough of this shitty little party.'

Darren shrugged. He was staying, unfortunately.

As they stormed off, slightly shoving me as they went, I heard one say, 'I couldn't see his face.' Then there was the sound of a glass bottle exploding against a wall.

'If you go down to the woods today, be sure of a big surprise,' said Sam.

Everyone chuckled.

'Hey, it *is* Halloween!' said Jack.

More laughter. But no one went into the forest any more.

Sam addressed everyone: 'And now inside for the big show. Let's go!'

I ambled inside with everyone else, and it was only as I entered the conservatory that Jack said, 'You're on. We know you'll amaze everyone.'

'What? Right now?' Fear and excitement fought for control of my brain. 'You must be kidding!'

Jack introduced me as 'The Next David Blaine' and Sam threw me a pack of cards, which I dropped. About five people, including Caroline, clapped; most jeered, including Darren. I regretted not having a chance to prepare the pack in advance.

I had rehearsed the patter a thousand times in front of the mirror at home so went on to autopilot with Ethan, my first volunteer: 'Go on, pick a card . . . Good choice . . . Hold it up for everyone else but don't let me see it . . . Put it back, anywhere you like . . . Let me give the pack a really good shuffle.' All of the time I was cutting and shuffling the pack. All false shuffles, of course. The real skill is to keep track of a card and then make it appear when you want.

'And . . . is this your card?' I had thrown three cards on to the table and turned over the middle one.

'Yeah,' said Ethan, 'that's it. How the hell did you do that, man?'

'It's a set-up,' someone yelled from the back.

'OK, step forward,' I said, offering the pack to the guy who had heckled. 'Look at the cards, count the cards, examine the cards – muddle them up as much as you like.

And then pick one. Don't let me see it.'

Of course, I didn't have to see the card, just keep track of it in the pack again. I put my fingers to my forehead as if to focus my magical powers.

'Now I'm going to lose it inside the deck by giving it a really good shuffle, mixing it up, making it random.' The pack went backwards and forwards between my hands, *apparently* being shuffled. 'Come closer,' I said, 'so that you can see I'm not cheating.' The crowd – *my* crowd – edged forward.

I tapped the pack on the table. 'I have no idea what your card is,' I said. 'But maybe the pack knows.' And when I spread the deck out on the table, just after the middle there was one card face up – the card he'd chosen.

There was a cheer. After that, even a quick fancy shuffle brought applause; they roared when I sent the cards through the air from one hand to the other.

I did a couple more tricks but I didn't want to start boring them.

'And now, ladies and gentlemen, my final trick. I will do something that the greats of magic have *never* achieved. The Great Lafayette, Derren Brown – *none* of them can do this, at least, not at *sixteen years old*.' It was like a real magic show. 'I will identify an object chosen while I'm out of the room.' I scanned the audience. 'For this, I need a volunteer.'

A lot of hands went up, but I had to pick Blake. He knew the trick; he knew how to play along as my stooge.

Blake helped by putting his hand up, but then someone suggested Sam and Jack, and a chant started: 'Sam and Jack! Sam and Jack!' Soon everyone joined in, apart from Blake, who understood that I was getting into trouble. Without someone who knew the code that guided me to what had been chosen, I was going to look a complete idiot after all.

Despite this, I went ahead, desperately thinking of a way out. After I left the room (Head Boy Mark volunteered for the role of 'reliable witness' to make sure I didn't peek), an obscure object was chosen in silence. 'Don't look at the object,' I said when I returned, frantically praying that Blake would look straight at it, but he shrugged and screwed up his face: the object was so obscure that I'd never get it by chance.

'And don't even think about it – that helps me!' I said, looking at Ethan, desperately hoping that he would give me a clue, but he was oblivious to the fact that I was looking for one. 'Ethan – I can also read your perverted thoughts!' I still had the entire room under my control, but knew that embarrassment was near.

'Let's hear it for Ben!' said Sam. Everyone cheered and the Twins came over and shook my hand theatrically.

'The pressure's back on,' said Jack.

Silence returned.

I made a great play of considering objects that were 'cold', and then ones that were slightly warmer and closer. Finally, complaining about the heat, I tipped out the pack and ran my hands over the upturned cards. 'Ouch – *this* one burns me,' I said, and lifted up the King of Hearts.

The room erupted into cheers. Darren shouted: 'Lucky, lucky bastard!'

'Thank you ladies and gentlemen,' I said. Now, that's *real* magic!'

Blake came over. 'I can't believe I've seen real magic for the first time,' he said. 'How did you get away with that?'

Sam's handshake, the crowd behind him, and the words 'Caroline's suit'; then Jack with 'King'. I was never sure why they didn't just tell me outright. Maybe they wanted an extra layer of mystery to show that we were in the same club; maybe they were genuinely worried about being overheard – I tried it in the mirror the next day, and you don't have to move your lips to say those words.

'Magicians must have some secrets,' I said. But The Twins had been the real magicians. Without them, I wouldn't have had the faintest idea what to find.

If an evening had ever changed my life for the better, this was it. Lots of people I'd never spoken to came over and slapped me on the back.

Over the noise, Jack shouted, 'There's plenty still to drink!' and slowly everyone dispersed.

Perhaps an hour later, The Twins encouraged everyone to the front of the house for the fireworks. I went forward with Ethan and Anna and we stood at the top of the sixty-foot cliff. I just about restrained myself from telling them about the abseiling.

'I love fireworks,' drawled Ethan. 'I love the ooh and the ahhhh, man. I love the whizz and the bang. Do you like a whizz and a bang, Anna?'

I liked Anna. She wasn't intimidated by anyone, and Ethan would never normally have been cheeky with her. 'If your little sparkler comes anywhere near me, I'll snap it in half,' she said.

At that moment, a firework shot up from the bottom of the cliff, seeming to pass just in front of our noses, and then shattered in the sky above us. After four small zippy ones, there was another rocket that exploded twice and lit up the mountainside. Then nothing. Ethan started to clap ironically and whispered to me that it wasn't exactly New Year's Eve on the Thames. Anna turned away. A few others muttered. For a party so fancy in other ways, it'd been a poor display.

'Better than nothing,' I said, determined to be loyal to The Twins.

Suddenly a firework soared up from Cormorant Holm, the island that was roughly in the middle of the Lake between Timberline and Compton Village. It was a clump of trees and knotty grass surrounded by boulders with a 'Private Property – Strictly No Mooring' sign on the side. I had rowed past with Will a few times when we were little, before my accident, but had never gone further than knocking Mrs Winter's rowing boat against the rocks. Will used to race his dad out to it, round it and back in their small yachts.

There was another firework, and another. Soon there were dozens, and the sky was a riot of colours reflected in the shimmering mirror of the lake. Red, pink, yellow and blue fell like exploding flowers. For a finale, a burst flew up from Cormorant Holm at the same time that others shot past us from the bottom of the cliff.

Silence.

Then we cheered.

'Man, that is the coolest thing that has ever happened in this dark corner of the universe,' said Ethan.

The Twins were besieged with compliments and questions. 'That was amazing!' – 'Who let them off?' – 'How did they get on the island?' – 'Do you do this sort of thing often?'

I said the same things.

It emerged that Cormorant Holm belonged to Timberline, and that The Twins' parents had arranged for the display.

'We're just really happy that everyone has been so great to us,' said Sam and Jack repeatedly.

In all of this I didn't hear anyone apart from Darren complain about them being poncey rich kids. Given the fireworks, magnificent house, abundant food and drink, people could easily have been antagonized rather than hooked. But The Twins wore tatty trainers and slightly frayed jeans and were content not to have the last word. 'You've got me there,' they might say, or 'I lose – how could I be such an idiot?' I didn't just admire them; I was in awe.

Later in the evening, after most people drifted away, I ended up with about ten others in the conservatory, the scene of my earlier success, arms outstretched over seats. Jack stood behind the others and nodded his head slightly to one side, very subtly indicating the door. I said something about needing the toilet and followed him out. But instead of going left, we turned right into an old-fashioned study.

Jack locked the door. The room was lined in dark wood with traditional landscape paintings of Lake Hintersea to the left and rows of books behind the desk.

'What's going on, mate?' I asked.

'I think we've a Challenge of bringing Mark "I'm-too-sexy-for-your-party" Roberts down a bit. Besides, he's with your girl,' said Jack.

Drinking a few beers had shifted the boundaries of common sense in my brain. 'Yeah – he's been annoying me all evening,' I said. He had been poking his nose in where it really wasn't wanted, interfering when I was helping Blake, annoying me with heavy policing of what was *my* magic performance.

Jack produced a small blue and white packet with *Ex-Lax* written on it: *Stimulant Laxative*.

'These will produce an explosion of turd. Are you on?'

I smiled.

'The best Challenges are the ones that bring justice,' said Jack.

'Yeah, I'm in,' I said, showing Jack two fists in celebration and then slapping his hand in a high-five.

'The little shit will be streaming with shit before he knows it,' whispered Jack as he draped his arm round my shoulder.

'But how do we get him to swallow them?' I asked.

'You're the magician,' said Jack. 'Let's grind up a few and slip them in his drink.' He handed me a paperweight from the desk and popped the pills out of their plastic container for me to crush. After three, I asked how many would be sensible.

'Don't be such a wimp,' said Jack. 'Here's two more.' He tore a page out of a notebook on the desk and brushed the powder inside. 'Sam and I will distract the others while you drop it in his drink.'

As we turned to go, I noticed that to the right of the door there was an old painting of a man in a Victorian suit. 'There,' I said, struck by the picture. 'He looks the same as your dad.' I was drawn in by the eyes – dark brown, intense, mesmerizing – the same eyes that The Twins had. There was a little bar underneath: *Samuel John Thatcher, Ward of Hintersea*.

'He's a great-great-grandfather or great-uncle or something,' said Jack. 'I think he's in books about the area. Never mind about him.'

'Cool in a way, though. Maybe that's why I thought I recognized your father,' I said. *Ward of Hintersea*? It sounded vaguely familiar. I remembered later that there's reference to it on one of the information boards on the far side of Ward's Fell.

It was easier to get the Ex-Lax powder into Mark's drink than I thought. Sam waited until Mark was standing up and then called him out of the room, which meant that he put his beer down on a table by the door, where there were some unopened cans. I hesitated for a second, but then went over and poured in the powder while Jack spoke to the others.

'We're going to play Spin-the-Bottle-Challenge,' he said, setting out the simplest rules of the game with amusing examples; at the same time, I swilled Mark's beer around with one hand and opened a can for myself with the other.

Seconds later, Sam returned with Mark, who was holding a bottle. The forfeit in the game was to drink some whisky.

I failed in a Challenge (to eat a bar of soap) and was surprised by how much a mouthful burned my insides as I gulped it down. I felt dizzy.

'My Challenge is for Mark to drink all that beer in one go,' Sam said, about four Challenges in.

Mark pretended to limber up and then drank it all, including the tablets, while we all chanted, 'Drink! Drink! Drink!'

A few goes later, Jack spun, and the bottle ended up pointing very definitely at me. 'Ben's Challenge,' he said, 'is to snog the person the bottle points at next time.' But Jack didn't even bother spinning the bottle, he just set it down so that it pointed directly at Caroline, who was next to him, and then fell back laughing.

Caroline just raised her eyebrows and smiled wryly.

'Jack!' I slurred. 'I can't believe you've done that.' I had drunk too much. Either I was moving or the room was, and it felt like both.

'And it has to be a good five seconds,' Jack added.

I moved across the floor on my hands and knees, and leaned forward, awkwardly aware (as I'm sure Caroline soon was) that I had never kissed a girl before. I remember our mouths clumsily opening and closing, but never at times that seemed to match. I fell into a giggling heap afterwards, unable even to look at Caroline, let alone speak to her.

As the others laughed at me, I turned to Mark. 'I'm

sorry,' I said. I think it was about kissing his girlfriend; perhaps I half had in mind what was in store for him.

'It's Caroline you need to apologize to,' he said with good humour. 'I'm not worried.' I hated his easy-going confidence almost as much as the laughter in the room and grinned joylessly for a few seconds.

It was the middle of the night, long after Blake had been collected, that we stood on the gravel at the front of the house and saw the headlights of two taxis slowly rise up the driveway to the house. I had only been in a taxi a couple of times before, but The Twins had insisted on paying, even though it cost extra for the cars to drive all the way from town.

Mark looked back at the house and said he needed the toilet.

'Hey, just one more second,' said Sam. 'Listen to this . . .'

'No,' Mark said through clenched teeth, one hand on the seat of his trousers. 'I've really got to . . .'

I even stood in his way. 'Hold on, mate,' I said. 'The cabs are coming.'

He was now wriggling and confused, torn between a polite dash for the toilet inside and an embarrassing rush for bushes.

'Oh hell . . .' He swore again. There was nowhere close enough for him to hide. The taxis had arrived at the top of the drive, blazing their headlights towards us – the house was lit – the garage was still open, lights on – as if we were on a stage. The forest was at the far end of the garden, a short dash earlier in the evening, but Mark was now in no condition to run.

Caroline was fairly sympathetic at first. 'Just hurry up, Mark,' she said. 'It's time for us to get going.'

There was a ripping sound as wind came first, and then Mark started to limp towards the forest, his hands covering his backside as brown liquid seeped through his trousers. He moved more slowly, struggling on. Then, as he turned the corner to head along the lit path, some liquid dribbled down from the bottom of his trousers on to his socks and shoes.

There were cries of disgust from the onlookers. 'Can't he control himself better than that?' someone said. From where we were, even though we were outside, we could smell it.

'Mark – this is gross. *Not* a good end to the party,' spat Caroline, hands on her hips.

Mark had turned the corner, but we could hear the sounds of violent, overwhelming diarrhoea.

'That idiot's not coming in my car!' shouted one of the

taxi drivers, casting a huge shadow as he stood in front of his car's headlights. 'The bloody drunken yob!'

'He doesn't sound well,' said Sam. 'Let's be brave and see if we can help.'

Caroline didn't move at first, but was encouraged forward. 'I *told* him to stop drinking,' she sighed – especially beautiful, I thought, in her anger.

'He was knocking back that whisky,' said Jack. 'I guess it's hard to know your limits.' He looked at Caroline and pushed his lips together in apparent sympathy.

Mark had hidden round the back of the garage, behind the first trees, but The Twins led us to him. Our appearance added humiliation to injury. Mark had lowered his trousers and his boxer shorts were covered in mess.

'We'll leave you to it and come back in a bit,' said Jack. 'Come on, guys, it's not right for us to see Mark like this.'

'Thanks,' groaned Mark, trying to hide what he could.

'And I thought you were different to the others!' Caroline said, before being beaten back by the stench and storming off to a taxi.

As he walked me over to the car that Caroline was in, Sam pulled me close and breathed in deeply.

'The sweet smell of revenge,' he said. 'The sweet smell of a completed Challenge.'

FIVE DAYS TO GO

✏️ Draft Email

To:	
Cc:	
Subject:	The Past

Someone else has to know the whole truth.

'Christmas Eve, 2016. The middle of London, next to Big Ben.
Midday,' he said. Then I watched him disappear into the
woodland. With anyone else, they'd be empty words.

It was so far in the future I thought we'd never get here.

I came close to telling you everything when we went to Compton
for Gran's funeral. You mentioned the view from the houses
in Compton across Lake Hintersea and how it must be full of
memories. 'Yeah,' I said. Just *Yeah* – not *I can remember what we
did as if it was yesterday.* Not *I can remember the faces of those
who died.*

Someone else has to know the truth in case it all goes wrong.

I'm not sure when it all started to change. Maybe that night at the party. It was the first time I'd set out to hurt someone else.

Now you see |

OCTOBER 2011
AUTUMN LEAVES

The next morning, Saturday, I was woken by the grumble of the postman's van outside. I strode down the stairs in pyjamas feeling like a different, bolder, more significant person. 'Hi, Gran,' I said. 'I'm up. Just getting a bowl of cereal.'

'You've only just got back,' she said from the front room. 'I heard you arrive about four a.m. I was worried sick!'

I flicked through the letters on the mat with my bare toes. Immediately, the world was spinning around my feet: I could see the words 'Benny (Private)'. No surname.

My gran could easily have got there first; had it arrived on a weekday when I was at school, she certainly would have. After glancing to make sure my gran couldn't see, I quietly ran my finger between the seal and the envelope, opening it with terrifying ease. It was written on the same type of card as before; the handwriting was Will's. My chest ached. Energy faded out of me.

I'm still fine. Don't worry.

Im actully writing because I want us to be friends.

I'mve had to have some secrets from you. I'll send one more
   letter soon.

Then everything will make sense.

I'm much closer than you think.

I'm even trusting you now. Please please please keep this a
   secret.

Will

I swore through gritted teeth.

'Benny, what's going on?' said my gran from the front room.

I screwed up my face and ran taut fingers through my hair. 'Oh, nothing,' I said, searching for a lie. 'I just whacked my toe on the . . . step. I don't think I want breakfast any more.' I did feel a bit queasy.

'You should have been more careful last night,' she said. 'Being out that late isn't good for you.' Then a mutter: 'I hope you weren't drinking alcohol.'

As before, I took the card upstairs. But this time I didn't cry.

Even with The Twins, I still missed Will so much that it hurt.

*

I've had to have some secrets from you.

Will hadn't been the same in the month before he was killed.

We had discovered the world together and had no secrets. Then something changed. He would go off in his boat or on his bike without telling me. I sometimes found him deep in thought, doodling. He fell asleep in a lesson.

'Will, what's going on?' I asked more than once. 'Wassup, mate?'

He was evasive: 'Nothing to worry your little head about . . .'; or: 'Benny, you're not my mother, stop nagging, give it a rest . . .'

The police listened at the start, then gradually lost interest. No one else had noticed it; but I was sure that I knew Will better than anyone.

I read the letter again and told myself to think logically. What if Will *was* alive? That would be *incredible – the biggest story in the history of the world* – and *totally* impossible. He was put in a coffin and lowered into the ground: I was there, just behind his parents, in the cemetery in Lancaster.

It was possible, in theory, that the notes were written by Will in the time between his abduction and death – but

89

these didn't read like letters sent from the dank den of an evil sicko. And they couldn't have been 'caught up in the post' (my gran's explanation for anything that was slow to arrive from Royal Mail): that was a mad idea – though not as mad as the idea that he was alive. And why not email? Will always emailed or sent a text.

Who the *hell* was posting the letters?

And why shouldn't I go to the police? Surely if Will was asking for help he would be desperate for police involvement? The warning about not telling anyone – that didn't sound like Will. Why didn't he just come out and tell me who had taken him?

There were only two people I could trust: The Twins. They didn't count as people who were not to be told.

'Benny,' my gran called from downstairs. 'Are you going to come in and see me?'

'I'm just getting dressed,' I half lied as I dropped the second note into Will's Box and searched for something to wear.

My gran could tell that something was wrong, but suspected a hangover. 'Are you sure everything is OK?' she said softly. 'Maybe you're learning a lesson after last night's party?'

'I think I'm a bit tired,' I said. 'Late night.'

I tried to keep the letter out of my head, but it kept welling up: *Im actually writing because I want us to be friends . . . I'm much closer than you think . . . Please please please keep this a secret.* Round and round it went.

'Too tired to take the church newsletter round?' she asked. It was the last Saturday of the month again. 'You could do with some fresh air.' The sun streamed in through the net curtains.

For once, walking around the village seemed appealing. It would remind me of real life and real death, rather than the stupid (fake) notes from Will.

I started with Mike Haconby's house, partly because I could see that his van was out. Bullseye barked aggressively as I wandered up the path. As soon as I put the newsletter through the door there was a snarl and it was ripped from my hand. 'Bullseye! Shut up, you stupid dog!' I said, kicking the door slightly. 'Shut up!' I swore at him.

I paused outside the churchyard and remembered the ambulance taking Will's body away on the morning after he was found. He lay there all night on the shore of the Lake under the white tents as experts picked around him with tweezer-like detail. 'Did you see anything? Did you hear anything? Anything at all?' the policeman had

91

asked. It was under 400 yards from my gate to Will's body.

It was a million-to-one chance that the body had been washed up a few steps from where Will had left his bike.

For a time, I had hovered on the edge of being a suspect. Maybe we had had a fight? There *had* been an argument, after all. Maybe a game went wrong? My clothes were taken away for forensic analysis.

(It was Will's mother's testimony that proved I had nothing to do with it. The Caplings' kitchen was on the Lane side of their house, so that their sitting room had the view of the Lake. 'I was standing at the sink,' Mrs Capling said, 'and saw Benny come out of his house and call for my dear William.' She broke down in tears after almost every sentence. 'William wasn't there. He was cycling round in circles the way that he always did. And then I looked up and my boy wasn't there.')

I stared at the church; an old, natural-stone building with a tower, the graveyard on its left. For the first time in a year, I put my hand on the gate to the church and pushed it open. *Will must have done this*, I thought. *He went through this gate. Just like this. He must have been pushing his bike, or maybe he nudged the gate and cycled through.*

There were gravestones on either side of the path, and I glanced at them as I walked in.

Edward Turnbull, beloved husband of . . .

Catherine Walker (1881–1963) . . .

Rest in Peace . . .

With the Lord . . .

Each step took me nearer.

There were fresh flowers and a small wooden cross in the distance, close to where Will's body was found, and I walked down towards the Lake. The Winters' jetty and the rowing boat came into view. I looked across the Lake, past Cormorant Holm, all the way to Timberline on the other side. Lakeside House peered down on me.

'Will, why did you write those letters?' I muttered, looking at the simple wooden cross. 'Why did you come *here*?' The flowers, wild ones that I'd seen a thousand times in the nearby fields, were fresh and neat. *I wonder who . . .*

I looked up in shock as Mrs Winter came into my peripheral vision, about twenty yards away. 'Sorry,' I said, my voice a little high and unsteady as I stood bolt upright. 'I didn't see you.'

'Hello, my *darling*,' she said as she slipped closer. 'I haven't seen you here before.'

Over her shoulder I could see a break in the hedge: there was a gate from the churchyard into her garden. 'No,' I admitted. 'This is the first time I've been able to get myself in here.' I looked around at the gravestones – death all around, most of it old, but some of it in new black marble.

'I think about young William often. He was such a dear, dear darling.' Mrs Winter looked down at the flowers. 'He's remembered by those who held him dear. He's not far away from us.'

'I think about him every day,' I said. I immediately wanted to leave. There was nothing more to say.

'He still cares for you as well,' she said, her pale green, unblinking, watery eyes glaring at me. 'Just as your mother does.'

It was the sort of thing that people had been saying. 'I'm sure he does, yes.' I exhaled once, to hint at an 'Oh dear' conclusion, and held out the penultimate newsletter from my pocket.

'He has not settled yet, you know,' she continued, her eyes still staring, but unfocused. 'He still reaches out to you.'

I encountered some of this nonsense soon after Will died. Even in a sensible part of the world there are cranks who pester the police with theories and messages. 'Do you mean from the spirit world?' I asked. My eyebrows were raised, mildly mocking; all I could think of was the letter.

'My darling, the spirit world and this world are not

separated like night and day – we are in twilight. He had to have some secrets from you, but soon everything will make sense.' Mrs Winter blinked and looked down at the flowers.

I'mve had to have some secrets from you . . . Then everything will make sense.

'What did you just say?' I blurted.

'Just what I've heard,' said Mrs Winter. 'I hear things.'

What the hell? It must have been a coincidence. I couldn't believe I was saying: 'Mrs Winter, he *is* dead, isn't he?'

She laughed loudly. 'What do you mean by "dead"? He isn't *settled*, if that's what you mean. But he wants to be settled. Maybe he needs your help?' Her voice was ghostly and thin, and I wondered if she was going to go into a trance.

Bonkers after all, I thought. I feared I was also going slightly mad, seeing connections where there were none. 'Anyway,' I said, making to move on. 'Thank you for putting the flowers here. That was very nice of you.'

'My darling, I have no reason to want to put flowers here.' She chuckled and shook her head slightly.

'But they're new. They're the ones that grow round here in the fields,' I said.

'Yes, fresh every single day. My *daaaaahling*, I see them brought in while you're all asleep.' It was hard to tell whether she was back in the real world or about to claim that they appeared paranormally or she did it while possessed by a spirit being.

'So how do they get here, then?' I asked, cynicism leaking into my voice.

There was now a hard edge to Mrs Winter's words: 'They're brought in by that Mr Haconby.' But her bitterness disappeared as quickly as it came, and she cooed: 'But I would do the same, my darling, if I were in his dreadful position.'

'I must get going,' I said, staring ahead. Lake Hintersea, creature-like, lapped the shoreline ahead of me; I imagined Will's body, gently rocked by the waves. My brain was in a haze. 'I didn't know that.'

'It's difficult to know everything,' she said. 'Even if you want to.'

I shook myself to my senses and glanced around at Lakeside House, glimpsing a figure in the central turret section at the very top, the Lantern Room that could be seen from miles around. The low November sun glinted off binoculars. I drew my breath in – Mrs Winter must have noticed – but the shape slipped back and I

96

could only see grey-tinged glass.

Mrs Winter smiled. Her teeth were greyish-brown, as if she had drunk too much tea. 'Trust me, *darling*,' she said. 'Follow William's footprints towards the distant sound, and there you will find the truth.' She had spoken in riddles before; now she seemed possessed.

'Thank you, Mrs Winter,' I said, the newsletter dropping to the ground between us. 'I really must be on my way . . .'

'That Easter went quickly,' she said, louder, as I walked away.

'Thank you, Mrs Winter!' I was striding away.

'The autumn leaves remind me of his hair,' she croaked.

I let the church gate swing shut behind me. 'Mad, stupid old cow,' I said to myself. But then I saw Mike Haconby's house: I said the words aloud: 'I hope for your sake that you had nothing to do with it . . .'

Mike Haconby's van was back. As I passed, Bullseye barked frantically.

I lay on my bed and closed my eyes. 13:23 by the bedside clock. Bullseye was still barking. *Why has this come back at the time it should be going away?* I concentrated on breathing in through my nose and out through my mouth, just as they had taught me when I couldn't sleep in the weeks after Will's death.

Slowly, I drifted into an uneven doze that was always in danger of tipping into waking. The dream came.

Will circled the road on his bike. The lane was thick with light brown autumn leaves.

Bark-bark-bark.

There was a man in a black cloak, carrying a scythe, his face as smooth as a pebble – completely featureless. His features came together like a jigsaw. It was Mike Haconby's face, but wrong, as if some of the sections had been forced into the wrong place.

No – it was a mask . . . There was someone underneath . . . He was tugging at his chin, about to peel it off.

Bark-bark-bark.

I looked at the book in my hand.

No: the face. Look at the face!

Bark-bark-bark.

I opened the book.

It's moving. Oh my God. It's not paper. It's alive! It's barking. There's something secret and important inside.

Bark-bark-bark.

I screamed as I awoke.

*

13:41. I sat on the side of the bed, rubbed my eyes, and heard the creaking floorboards and light steps that warned of my gran slowly climbing the stairs.

'Benny – I heard a shout. Are you OK?' she asked.

'Hold on, I'm not . . . ready. I'm just, er, getting stuff on,' I said.

'You do worry me sometimes,' she croaked.

On autopilot, I pulled down Will's Box and the back of his Rough Book caught my eye. There was a picture of a dog with a target, a bit like the RAF symbol, drawn on its side. An arrow was sticking into the middle of the target and some inky blood-like droplets below.

Bark-bark-bark.

I had never thought about it before. *Bullseye.*

I flicked through but couldn't see any other dog-like creatures. A sheep, a dragon, a poorly drawn tortoise – but no dog.

'Are you going to come downstairs to get something to eat?' asked my gran.

There was a mystery to be solved, and The Twins would help me to crack it. They always knew what to do.

I pushed Will's Box back into its place at the top the wardrobe.

Attachment

NOVEMBER 2011
AT THE MOUNTAINTOP

The Twins had never been to my house. To be honest, I was a bit embarrassed. My bedroom was tiny compared to The Twins' five-star hotel-style suites.

The Twins influenced me in a way that even Will hadn't: the way I spoke, my clothes (T-shirts at every opportunity), my desire to laugh at jokes and compliment people on what they achieved. 'Those boys make you much nicer' – even my gran said that, and she was suspicious of 'the youth of today'. I also had lots of new friends, all of them fairly normal people. Ethan and Anna sent me texts and I checked Facebook several times a day.

One remaining problem was that Darren Foss was still unpleasant to me every now and again, mainly by barging into me and saying, 'Watch yourself, Ben,' or, 'I didn't see you there' – that sort of crap. Blake had worse treatment.

It was on the first Sunday afternoon in November, a week after I found Will's second note, that I received a text:

> When you gonna show
> us around compton j&s

I almost sent one back straight away, but waited about fifteen minutes, just to appear busy:

> How bout half 2

They replied immediately:

> Ok c u

During an anxious week I had looked for the right opportunity to tell them about the letters from Will. Now was my chance.

I was outside on my bike, circling around just as Will did before he was taken, thinking about why he decided to cycle to the churchyard, when I saw The Twins and one other person cycle round the corner by Lakeside House. It didn't occur to me that they would bring someone else, and I certainly wasn't expecting Darren Foss. His unexpected arrival made my heart sink.

'Hi, Ben,' Sam said, skidding to a halt next to me. 'I hope you don't mind that we brought Darren. We thought it might make things cool after the party. And we're in the same Physics class. But if it's a problem . . .'

'Hi, Darren,' I said, looking down at the road.

'How's it hanging?' Darren sniffed, and cracked his knuckles. 'I'm sorry about the other night, if I actually did something wrong, which I probably didn't.'

'Yeah, OK,' I said. 'I'm sorry too.'

It wasn't simply that Darren was there – though, believe me, his presence made me feel depressed – it was that I would have to share The Twins, and there's no way I could mention the letters from Will.

'Right! Come with me,' said Jack. He rode a few yards and then stopped outside the church – it was opposite there that the signpost promising Ward's Fell pointed across a field.

As always, my eyes were drawn to the graveyard. I was taken back to police cars and the uncontrollable crying of Will's parents. I never saw the body but had dreamed of him lying in Lake Hintersea waves underneath white CSI tents.

'Is that where the boy was killed?' asked Darren, feet planted either side of his bike. 'Let's have a look.'

'I'm not sure if that's where he was killed,' I muttered, unmoving. 'But that's where his body was found.' It was one of the mysteries of the case. There was no sign of a struggle in the graveyard – his bike had been neatly propped against a gravestone, taken away for analysis and never returned; as obvious to me as a tooth plucked from a mouth, the missing gravestone showed exactly where Will's bike had been left. At the far end of the churchyard, it was possible to see Lake Hintersea and the spot where Will was found.

'You go in. I'm happy here.' I shrugged.

The words in the notes from Will started going around in my head and I wondered if Darren was secretly having a good laugh.

'In that case, we don't want to go in either,' said Jack.

'I'm staying here with Ben,' said Sam.

'There's no need for any more detective work,' said Darren. 'We *all* know who did it. Just no one is prepared to do anything about it. And you two agree with me. You said so.' He was looking to The Twins for support.

Sam started. 'It's what everyone thinks, Ben. My dad even heard that it's not the first time Mike Haconby has been involved with missing kids, but they had to keep it quiet for fear of wrecking the case.'

'Do you *really* believe *that*, guys?' I said, addressing The Twins and forgetting about Darren. 'That's just rumour; it's just the sort of thing people say to make mud stick.' I remembered my gran using the same words. I'm not sure if I still believed them.

'I don't want to talk about it here,' said Sam, looking along the road to where Mike Haconby lived. He lowered his voice. 'Our dad said that it's true.'

'I don't know why you're protecting the weirdo who killed someone who was *supposed* to be your friend,' sneered Darren.

I thought about grabbing my bike and riding off, leaving them all behind – even The Twins.

But suddenly Jack's hand was on my elbow as if he was transmitting good energy. His eyes were sad and understanding. 'Come on, let's go up there,' he said.

Sam was already pointing. 'Yeah! Is it right there's a cave?' His finger reached out towards Ward's Fell, the 2,790-foot-high 'mountain', the twenty-third highest in England, behind Compton Village. 'The Challenge is to walk to the top in a straight line.'

The Twins controlled my mood, as they always did. I liked the use of the word 'Challenge' and had begun to use it myself. 'Yeah, good Challenge,' I said.

Darren's voice was lifeless and slightly sarcastic: 'Yeah. OK. It looks really scary. I might wet my pants.'

It was just about possible to go straight up Ward's Fell

in a straight line, over stone walls, through a band of trees that hid rocky crags, then scrambling over grass and stones too steep for sheep, but despite living in Compton Village all of my life, I had only gone up that way once. The signposted path was much easier, but circled round the mountain and took ages. And Sam was right: near the top of the mountain there used to be a small slate mine, rather like a cave. I remembered Will sitting in the entrance when we walked up there.

We cycled down the path that headed across the fields, then left our bikes in undergrowth behind a couple of trees.

Jack's leg seemed to have returned to normal, though sometimes, perhaps, I saw him twitch a little. It certainly didn't slow him as we strode through ferns and nettles, and scrambled over walls and under barbed-wire fences.

The Twins were mad on cars and we chatted about *Top Gear*.

'It's important to know what your limits are,' said Sam.

'And there's only one way to find that out,' said Jack.

'You only know things have gone too far when they go too far,' Sam said. He then lunged forward and bundled Jack to the ground, playfully slapping the area on Jack's leg that had been injured.

'Come on, guys,' I said. 'You don't want to hurt him.'

'Don't worry, mate,' said Jack. 'We know when to stop.'

After we moved on, Darren talked about sex – the weird stuff that boys say when they don't know what they're going on about. He created a sort of punchline: 'I bet that's the sort of thing Ben enjoys.'

It wasn't quite like the bullying before, and for a time we all laughed, then it began to annoy me. Darren would say something perverted and simply add, 'I bet that's the sort of thing Ben enjoys.' I gazed down at the lake in the distance and breathed deeply. The afternoon was going wrong, just as I feared. At least Blake wasn't with us.

Without warning, both Twins stopped and turned to Darren. 'You're forgetting our deal,' said Jack.

'Say wha', bro?' said Darren, arms outstretched.

No one was laughing now.

Darren stood still, weighing something up, while The Twins and I walked on. Then he shouted after us, ''Kay. Whatever you say, dudes.'

We were now a few paces ahead and Sam pulled me right next to him and whispered in my ear: 'Don't worry, Ben, we know who you're really interested in, and we'll get you and Caroline together.'

I chuckled.

'Don't get pissed off by Darren,' whispered Jack from the other side. 'You trust us, don't you? It's you, Sam, and me. We all enjoy a Challenge. We're never outdone. Shame I didn't bring any Ex-Lax!'

After another hundred yards, we reached the entrance to the mine. 'Mine' is a big word for what was really just a dip in the hillside that someone had used as an excuse to dig out slate, making a few tunnels in the process.

We all had mobile phones with basic torch apps, but The Twins suddenly produced two Ledlenser torches from their rucksacks.

How did they know that we would end up here? It was as if they saw the road ahead before anyone else.

Someone had put in a metal door to try to keep people out of the tunnels beyond, but the chain was lying on the floor next to a rusty and broken padlock. The door had been bent and buckled slightly over the years and made a creaking sound as Jack pulled it back a few inches.

'How about a Challenge?' said Sam, peering into the darkness before switching on his torch.

'What d'ya mean? Like a dare?' asked Darren.

Darren wasn't in on the lingo. Great.

'Yeah,' Sam said. 'We'll go in and find the furthest wall . . .'

'And leave our initials,' Jack finished.

'Wicked,' I said. 'Our names'd stay there for ever.'

'There could be snakes in there, or monsters,' Darren mocked. He grabbed me and shook me slightly.

I wriggled free and went forward to look along Sam's torch beam. Other people had certainly been there before: there were discoloured beer cans and faded, damp sweet wrappers. Someone, probably years ago, had left the remains of a small fire. 'Let's go,' said Jack. With Sam in front of me and Jack behind, I felt safe.

We wandered in, no sound apart from the echo of our shoes scuffing. The floor was peppered with stones and bits of slate, and the tunnel wasn't straight, but The Twins' torches produced more than enough light for all four of us.

'See what it's like with the torches off.' It was my voice.

At this point in the tunnel, about twenty yards in, there was still a pale light from the open entrance behind us, but when we tried the same thing about ten paces on, round a slight left-hand bend, it was completely black.

The tunnel then veered ninety degrees left, and soon there were two forks – but we very quickly saw that the one on the right only went about five yards, so we came back: Sam, then me, then Jack, with Darren last.

The other way went further, maybe another fifteen

yards. 'I hope this rock isn't going to fall on us,' said Darren.

'Don't be an idiot,' said Jack. 'It's been here for a hundred years or whatever – it's not going to decide to collapse right now.'

Sam pressed his hand against the slate wall that ended the tunnel: 'And that's it. The end.' It was as if the miners had just lost interest one afternoon and decided to leave it jagged and incomplete, with barely enough surface for us to scratch our names.

As the torchlight wobbled around, I ran my hand over the floor of the tunnel, searching for something sharp enough to scratch my initials with. Eventually I found a shard of slate that nestled in my palm and could be pressed hard enough to leave a faint imprint on the stone. I scratched my initials: *B.A.C.* About eighteen inches away *DARREN* finished writing the six letters of his name. The Twins left no evidence that they had ever been there.

I was about to ask why when there were two clicks, less than a second apart. In an instant, it was pitch black.

'Wooooooo!' It was Darren. He cupped his hands over his mouth and spoke in a creepy voice: 'Ben – I am coming to get you!'

'Put them back on, guys,' I said.

There wasn't a sound. I slowly put my hands out and felt the clammy walls of the tunnel. Bizarrely, I then felt my own face and pulled my eyelids up to check that they were open. 'Hey, guys!' I was now shouting. 'Stop messing around!' I groped for my phone.

Suddenly, I was grabbed and a hand smothered my mouth. For a split second, I thought it was Darren, but the arm across my chest, the hand on my shoulder, the chest tight against my back, then the hair tickling my ear . . . Instinctively, I knew it was one of The Twins. It was as dark with my eyes closed as with them open.

'Yeah! Stop messing around!' Darren's voice boomed out of the darkness. 'I can't see a thing, you bastards.' He swore, then yelped, and I could hear the sound of his head being rubbed – I suppose he had knocked against the side of the tunnel. Then Darren shouted again, perhaps two paces away, maybe closer: 'Get off! What are you doing? You sicko!' Swearing. 'My phone! Give it back to me!' More swearing. 'Come back here! Now! You little shit!'

I was spun around 180 degrees, but the Twin stayed behind me and whispered: 'Walk, quickly. Trust me.' For the first few strides I was braced for impact, teeth clenched, terrified I would be driven head first into stone, but then I relaxed slightly and blindly trusted my guide. We must have gone about fifteen paces when I was turned sharply right, held still for a moment, then marched off again. This time we went slightly slower and I felt my arm graze against the side once or twice, but then grey daylight grew into distant shafts of sunshine.

'What the hell are you doing?' I said, keeping the same pace and looking forward.

'It's Jack. Keep going.'

I could see Sam ahead, standing in the entrance of the mine, the long chain dangling in one hand and a shiny padlock in the other. Yes – a shiny new padlock.

I squinted as we strode out of the tunnel. Jack leaned against the metal door, pushing it as tightly closed as possible, while Sam threaded the chain round the handle and round a metal hook screwed into the rock. The door fitted securely: for anyone inside, it must have blocked out all but paper-thin slithers of light.

'What the hell are you doing?' I said. 'Darren's still in there.'

The Twins laughed. 'We warned him,' Jack said.

'We said that if he did anything to you that we didn't like, we would put him in a bad place,' Sam added.

'I don't think he understood we meant it literally,' Jack concluded.

I stared at the door – it was chipped and dented, but there was no way it could be forced open.

'You're joking, aren't you?' I said. I was unsettled, scared, and excited as well. I nudged a few gravel-sized stones with my feet. My eyes darted from Sam to Jack, to the door, to the Lake in the distance, but my imagination was with Darren.

Sam put his hand on my shoulder. 'We did this for you. How long do you want him to stay in there?'

'I dunno,' I muttered. 'I didn't really want him there in the first place.' I think I was worried about getting into trouble.

'Perhaps we should let him out?' said Jack.

There was a shout from behind the door, then another, closer. We stared at the metal. I put my hand to my mouth. The Twins smiled. Then the metal shook and rattled.

'You bloody bastards,' Darren shouted. 'Let me out!' He beat his fist on the door. 'Let me out – I can't see a thing in here. I don't like it any more.'

Sam pulled Jack to him as they grinned.

There was a deep scream from inside. 'Please, please help me – please! I know you're there. Please!'

I went forward to the door. 'Darren, listen. This was just a joke, and to teach you a lesson. I've had enough of you pushing me around.' I couldn't hear anything from the other side of the door. 'You've done worse things to me than this.'

Darren spoke through his teeth: 'OK.'

Sam stood beside me. 'We want you to apologize to Ben. And we want it to sound good.' A silence followed that ended as Sam kicked the door hard.

'I'm very, very sorry,' said Darren.

'And I know I will suffer if I ever insult Ben again,' said Jack.

'I know I will suffer if I ever insult Ben again,' Darren chanted as if bored. He shook the door; the chain pulled tighter. 'Now let me out!'

Sam went close to the door and spoke in little more than a whisper: 'If we leave you, you'd never know if someone was passing, so you'd have to shout for hours, or days, even when you were tired and thirsty.'

Sam walked away from the door and was followed by Jack. I trailed after them, binding myself emotionally closer to them with each step. We didn't stop walking until we were away from the mine entrance and had the spectacular view of the Lake from the top of Ward's Fell. There was no one else in sight.

'Ben,' Sam said, 'we should leave him there longer. At

the moment he's an angry snake, waiting to strike. We have to tame him. We need to show him that we're in charge and he needs to respect you.' He pulled out the key to the padlock. 'It's your decision. You're intelligent.' The key was placed in my palm. 'You can let him out now, in a minute, or in an hour.' Sam put his mouth so close to my ear that I could feel his cheek against mine. 'Or never. Your decision.'

A few minutes earlier I would have rushed over and let Darren out. Now I put the key in my pocket. It wasn't just that I wanted to please The Twins; and it wasn't just that I could see Sam's logic. It was partly because I couldn't see or hear Darren. But that wasn't all: I felt the warm excitement of being in control over another person. The fuel that powers a bully burned within me.

'I think Darren needs to learn a lesson,' I said, walking a little way and sitting down on the grass. 'This is nothing compared to what he's done to me.' The final stage: justification for my actions.

'Stand up,' said Sam. 'And come over here.'

Like a puppet, I went over. Jack joined us, and we put our arms around one another and rested our three foreheads together. 'We're three brothers now,' Jack said.

'Three musketeers,' said Sam.

'Thank you,' I said. I had forgotten about Darren.

After we parted: 'Hey – catch!' Jack threw me a bar of chocolate, and then one to Sam. He threw to *me* first. Something had changed. Jack then reached into his rucksack a second time. 'Want a cigarette?'

After about an hour, as the sun began to dip down towards the hills on the far side of the Lake, I decided to go back and let Darren out. The Twins stood some distance behind.

'Help! Help!' Darren was calling.

'Shut up, Darren, I'm here with the key,' I said.

There was silence from the other side of the door as I calmly put the key in the padlock and threaded the chain through the loop.

'About time,' said Darren as he blinked in the light. Seeing that I didn't have The Twins with me, he growled in a low voice, full of anger: 'I'm going to kill you. I'm going to make you scream, *Benny*!'

I brought my fist up against Darren's chin so fast and hard that his head shot back like a snapped piece of wood. A second fist brought blood, and then, after he fell, I had my right hand round his neck on the ground. 'If you touch me again, I'm going to rip your throat out. Understand?'

'Yes,' he slurred through split lips. 'I'm going to leave you alone from now on.'

'What's my name?' I whispered.

There was something in his eyes I hadn't seen before. Fear. 'Ben,' he said.

'What's my name?' I shouted, slapping him.

'Ben,' he said, louder.

'This one is for Blake.' I hit him one more time, hard, striking nose and mouth together. Finally defeated, frightened to move, Darren covered his face with his hands.

I wonder what he saw in my eyes. Whatever it was, Darren didn't just stop bullying Blake and me. He hardly spoke to us again.

I walked back to The Twins. 'Well done, bro,' said Sam.

'There's one other person we need to bring into line,' said Jack. 'We have the Challenge of bringing to justice whoever murdered Will.'

I thought of the letters, of Mike Haconby's guilt, of how the police seemed to know it was him but couldn't prove it. 'Yeah,' I said. 'That's the main thing.'

Sam spoke louder, nearly a shout, as if he wanted someone high in the sky to hear. 'It is a Challenge. And we never, never, *never* fail in a Challenge.'

NOVEMBER 2011
GAME THEORY

The Twins were flesh and blood like the rest of us, but it wouldn't have surprised me if they'd turned out to be robots. They were never ill and never looked tired. When there was a Sixth Form photo taken under the trees by the Science Block, a shaft of light crept between the branches and fell, centre stage, on The Twins. I still have the picture: two hundred people, but two stood out. It was the little things. In History, while we were concentrating on Dr Richardson's text, Caroline accidentally nudged a pencil from the table and Sam's hand flashed out to catch it. There are a thousand stories.

The Twins even convinced coolest-of-the-dudes Ethan and no-nonsense Anna to become an item.

I felt guilty that I went for whole days without thinking about Will.

I began to spend a bit of time with Caroline. 'Hey, Ben, can you help me with this essay after break?' she said after one lesson. 'Jack says you really understand it.' We sat together over History books in the library. To begin with, I made her smile; before long, I made her laugh.

In the week after Darren was locked in the old mine, I again looked for opportunities to tell The Twins about Will's letters, but the time never seemed right. I also knew that I was going to sleep at their house on Friday night.

The Twins were left almost completely alone by their parents, who I never saw and had only heard a handful of times on the phone. I didn't really have a yardstick for how odd this was – my gran hassled me about the tiniest mess, but I knew that she was different, older, fussy. 'Dad's been in Zurich on legal business for three weeks,' said Sam, 'and Mum's down in London.'

To get to and from school, we took a small school bus that twisted its way round Lake Hintersea. But on the Friday evening of the sleepover, The Twins' dad collected us from school after driving up from Heathrow. His Mercedes E-Class stopped on double yellow lines outside the school.

'Get in,' he said immediately, with no other greeting. 'I'm going in there to the loo.' He nodded towards the main school building.

The Twins just said, 'OK.'

I wanted to call him by name but couldn't seem to remember the right one. Then my head was full of the portrait of *Samuel John Thatcher, Ward of Hintersea* that I'd seen the night of the party. 'Mr . . . um . . . Thatcher, you're parked on double yellows.' I had seen tickets slapped on cars before.

He gave a little snort. 'Lines on a road,' was all he said.

Being with The Twins made me confident and helpful. 'They sometimes give tickets.' The Twins' father, surely, would be like his sons. The apple doesn't fall far from the tree.

'Is that the worst that will happen?' He looked at me dismissively.

'Yes, I s'pose,' I muttered.

The teacher on duty strode over, eyes bright at the doubly wicked combination of posh car on yellow lines. 'Excuse me, is that your vehicle parked there?' she huffed.

'Yes,' Mr Thatcher said, and walked off into school.

Mr Thatcher had never told me his first name. He instructed The Twins with the cold control of a chess player moving pieces, but that didn't affect their mood one bit: their banter with me was as friendly as ever. I'd grown up knowing that my own father had separated himself completely from my life, so – secretly, horribly – I enjoyed that The Twins didn't seem to have a very close relationship with their dad.

*

At Timberline, as always, we went to one of their rooms. It happened to be Sam's, which I preferred as it had a huge piece of modern art on the ceiling – something I'd never seen done before. I threw myself down onto a beanbag and looked up at the splashes and swirls of colour. 'I think I see a camel sitting on a lily pad,' I mumbled, trying to make sense of the shapes.

I closed my eyes. The little pods inside the beanbag rustled as Sam arrived next to me. 'We've become great friends, haven't we?' he said.

'Yeah,' I replied. Friday nights before The Twins arrived were just like every other night: tea with my gran, perhaps some television, then upstairs to practise magic or play on the computer. 'Yeah.' I shrugged, pretending they weren't the most important thing to me, more important than magic, more important than Gran. More important than Will.

Jack moved to the other side, his shoulder leaning against mine. 'Can you *really* keep a secret?'

It was a question I was about to ask them. Will's letters were in my bag, waiting for the right time to be mentioned.

I sat upright. 'If the secret had to be kept, then yeah. Ab-so-lutely.' It was the sort of response The Twins would have given. 'Go ahead. Trust me.' I tried not to sound pleading.

'Ben: you're one of us,' said Jack. Again, The Twins' eyes: hardly any pupil, marbles, as hypnotizing as Kaa in *The Jungle Book*. 'We want you to know about, let's call it a . . . hobby that we have. It's nothing fancy, but we've set up a website that sets Challenges.' He stood up and wiggled the mouse on the computer desk next to his bed and the large computer screen blinked into life. The Challenge was written as a banner at the top of the page. 'The address is *thechallenge2*.' He gave me an 'It's-just-a-little-bit-of-fun' smile. 'Our family has always liked to set Challenges and play games.'

'A website? That's *amazing*.' But I wished they'd mentioned it before; I didn't like that any part of their life was secret from me.

Sam leaped up and joined his brother. 'It's a basic site. Put a traffic cone on a famous statue, bare your arse in front of Buckingham Palace – that sort of thing. Evidence is posted online.' He returned with two newspaper cuttings: *Internet Pranksters Paint Sheep Pink*. 'That – is *us*.' *Internet Craze Girl Returns Home*. The second story was about someone who had been away from home for forty-eight hours: she had disappeared (and reappeared) without warning 'because of an online game'. Near the end of the article there was a reference to a name: *The Challenge*.

'It started with us,' said Jack, 'but now it's basically a chat room for sharing dares. Perfecto!' He was tapping the screen. 'Now that's an awesome Challenge! An acid smiley flag in the weirdest place possible. A *classic*.'

THE CHALLENGE. I thought the banner behind Jack's bed was cool.

'Not all of the Challenges are online. On the night of the party it was a Challenge to get you and Caroline to kiss,' said Jack.

'You bastards,' I said. 'But thanks, guys!' We laughed. 'And I won't tell anyone . . .' *There's no one to tell*, I thought. *There's only really The Twins.*

'That's just one secret,' said Sam. 'In any case, you're a Challenger with us.' We slapped hands.

'There's something more,' said Jack. 'Something that's top secret. Something no one else knows.'

'You know I won't tell anyone. You know that I'm totally, well, loyal to you.' It didn't sound wrong, though it looks stupid written down. I almost said 'devoted'.

'If you told someone else, we'd have to kill you.' There was silence for a moment before they both burst out laughing. 'And you know we can't do that,' said Sam, 'because you're too important to us.'

'Thank God!' I chuckled.

'We sometimes set Challenges ourselves,' said Jack. 'And one of them involves you.'

'Me? Who has set the Challenge?'

'Now *that* would be telling,' Jack whispered. 'But every game needs a Games Master.'

I assumed that the Games Master was Sam or Jack – or both of them.

'It's to do with your friend, Will Capling,' said Sam. 'We know about Will. And our Challenge is to punish the man responsible.'

This was the moment. I reached in my bag and pulled out the two notes from Will. 'Guys, hold it. There's something I really have to tell *you*.' In my hands the letters looked insignificant; it would be easy to lose them and forget. 'I want you to see these.'

In silence, they read them a couple of times and swapped them over. I closed my eyes again and listened to their breathing and the tiny rustles of Will's notes:

Hi Benny. I'M NOT DEAD.

Everyone wants to know what happened to Me – I know that.

Look, I know I can trust you. Its important you dont tell

anyone at all. Definately not the police.

PLEASE just play along. Perhaps you'll want to tell Sylvie or my
   parents, but don't.
(Think of me whenever you eat a curliewurly. I'll be back.)
Will

And:

I'm still fine. Don't worry.
I'm actually writing because I want us to be friends.
I'mve had to have some secrets from you. I'll send one more
   letter soon.
Then everything will make sense.
I'm much closer than you think.
I'm even trusting you now. Please please please keep this a
   secret.
Will

Sam swore. 'Have you showed these to anyone?'

I explained that they were the only people to see them.
'They're probably fakes to creep me out . . .' I still wanted to
believe that Darren or one of his heavies was responsible.
After all, no notes had come in since I'd thumped him. 'But
the handwriting is right, and only Will would understand
the thing about the Curlywurly. It was a stupid joke we had.'

The Twins looked closely at the notes, smelt them, held them up to the light. 'No good for fingerprints,' Jack said slowly. 'Our hands have been all over them.'

'Any killer with half a brain would have worn gloves,' muttered Sam.

'You don't actually think they're genuine, do you?' I'd hoped that they would see a flaw – but instead they saw something else:

'I can't see a message in the second one,' said Sam. He tapped his index finger to his lips and then muttered random words from the note, tracing his finger down the page.

'Message? The stupid thing is that there *isn't* really a message,' I said.

'It's much clearer in the first one . . .' said Jack. He pointed at the start of the lines.

Hi Benny. I'M NOT DEAD.

Everyone wants to know what happened to Me – I know that.

Look, I know I can trust you. Its importent you dont tell
   anyone at all. Definately not the police.

PLEASE just play along. Perhaps you'll want to tell Sylvie or my
   parents, but don't.

125

'Oh my God,' I said, hands to my mouth.

'It was starting the sentence with *Everyone*,' said Sam. His finger slid down the page, pointing four times: H, E, L, and P.

HELP.

Why the hell hadn't I seen that? I was too busy reading the words to look at the letters. It changed everything.

Jack swore loudly and pointed at the second note. He was half talking to himself. 'I've got it. Look – the crossing out before the *ve*, and the *"actully"*, and the *even*, that's an odd word to put in – what the . . .' He swore again. 'Look at the second words! Look!'

I'm ~~s~~till fine. Don't worry.

Im **actully** writing because I want us to be friends.

I'~~mve~~ had to have some secrets from you. I'll send one more letter soon.

Then **everything** will make sense.

I'm **much** closer than you think.

I'm **even** trusting you now. Please please please keep this a secret.

SAVE ME.

'That must be done on purpose,' said Jack, waving the

note. 'That's absolutely bloody terrifying!'

'But why weren't they posted until now?' I raised my eyebrows. 'And why would a killer want to send them?'

Jack perched on the windowsill. 'I s'pose psychos are like that – taunting people, playing with the cops.'

'I still don't get it,' I said. 'Look – if you were being held by some lunatic and managed to get a letter out, you wouldn't just send a note saying that you were captured; you'd send *precise* instructions. If you're writing in code, you might as well put all the facts. Will wasn't stupid, he was really clever – you can see that – so why didn't he just tell me exactly where he was?'

After a silence, Sam spoke deliberately and slowly – ominously. 'Will must have thought you'd know exactly where to look. Somewhere very close.'

I thought of the view from my bedroom window. Two houses were opposite: Will's and Mike Haconby's. We saw Mike all the time; no one had threatened us more often; no one had been more of a suspect. 'When we went up the mountain, Darren said that you knew something about Mike Haconby – what's that? You said your dad knew he'd been involved with missing kids before, but the police couldn't prove anything.'

The Twins offered to take me to their dad.

*

It was Sam who knocked on the door to his study. Jack had been there first, I'm sure, but waited for his older brother. 'He'll answer when he's ready,' said Sam, his ear towards the door.

'Come in.' Mr Thatcher was wearing half-moon glasses and peering at a computer screen. 'Just wait.' He put his left hand up for us to be quiet and typed something with his right.

We stood like three naughty kids in front of the Head Teacher's desk.

'Yes?' he said, swiping off his glasses and pointing them at Sam.

Sam stood upright. 'Father –' yes, he said '*Father*' – 'are you able to tell us about the man who lives in Compton Village, Mike Haconby – the one who was involved in the disappearance of the boy earlier this year?'

We stood in silence as he pulled a legal-looking document from a filing cabinet and read it. The clock ticked thirty or forty times.

'Mr Thatcher,' I said, strengthened by being between The Twins, but my voice sounding reedy and pathetic. 'This is really important to me.'

'Ah,' he said. 'I'm told that there is no actual *proof* that

Mr Haconby killed Master Capling. No proof, at least, that would stand up in court.' Mr Thatcher flicked through the document. 'You see, the prosecution would be unable to disclose previous convictions.' He looked about a third of the way down the page. 'Mr Haconby served a few months in 1987 for Violent Disorder. In 1994 he went to prison for Possession of a Firearm with Criminal Intent. In 1997 he was jailed under the Offences Against the Person Act of 1861 – for repeatedly threatening to kill a university student who lived in the same street in Oldham. That jail time was immediately before Mr Haconby arrived in Compton Village. And it was three years before the *entirely* unconnected death of that same young man – who was found after a short disappearance, drowned in the Manchester Ship Canal.' He closed the file. 'He has certainly not lived a perfect life.' He put his glasses back on and stared at the screen.

No proof that would stand up in court. He has certainly not lived a perfect life.

'Thank you,' I said. As I turned, the painting of *Samuel John Thatcher, Ward of Hintersea* looked at me with the same rigid expression as Mr Thatcher.

Back upstairs, we discussed what had apparently happened to Will.

'Why would Will go off with him? And where the hell did he keep him for two days before he was found? And would Will have emerged from that unharmed apart from one blow to the head? He would have fought like a caged beast. And the cops tore that house apart. And why did he push him in the Lake?' I didn't stop to consider any one particular question. 'It just seems so needless and senseless and stupid.' I looked out of Sam's window, which overlooked Lake Hintersea. Compton Village's lights were pinpricks visible in the distance. I wondered if one of them was Mike Haconby's. 'What he did was evil.'

'I'm sure killers have their own logic,' said Jack.

We plotted our revenge in a terrifyingly calm way. Our discussion centred on how to take something important away from Mike. The dark, the whispers, the foggy judgement that comes after midnight – it all helped dissolve normal good sense.

The Twins saw it as a matter of simple justice. 'Let's think logically. We could say "an eye for an eye",' said Jack. 'He's killed; that means he thinks killing people is OK. But he's slaughtered an innocent boy. *We're* only thinking of killing a dog.'

Sam's voice was uncharacteristically high-pitched and

dismissive. 'It's just a dog. It's no different to a cow or a sheep, and we *eat* them. People hunt foxes, and they're basically dogs. It's just an animal.'

To me, killing a dog wasn't the same as a cow or a sheep. I didn't have any attachment to Bullseye – all he did was bark, and he probably would have bitten me given the chance – but even that aggression was a type of *character*, and it was personality that set Bullseye apart from farmyard animals. I think I would have agreed to killing, say, a budgie in a second. But a dog?

'We're balancing a dog's life against the life of your friend,' said Jack. 'And who knows, maybe Bullseye was used to capture Will in the first place?'

The police said Will hadn't been harmed in any way apart from drowning and a blow to his head, but I pictured him in the churchyard, unable to escape as Bullseye herded him towards a baseball bat. Guilt poured on to the creature.

'OK,' I finally agreed. 'Bullseye can't be happy living with him anyway – it'd be like putting him down.' I breathed out, feeling that I was no longer responsible for the decision. We were purely being logical. 'But we should do this in as painless a way as possible. It's not really Bullseye's *fault*. He can't help it.'

'Agreed,' said Sam. 'You're totally right. We can poison him. Easy.' And in that moment Bullseye's life was dismissed.

'Have you ever done anything like this before?' asked Jack.

I thought back to things I regretted. 'Probably not,' I said. Mark Roberts and Darren Foss were the only times I'd purposely hurt someone. But they deserved it, especially Darren. And Mark – that was innocent play.

It was 3.00 a.m. when we went to sleep in the same room, like brothers. I lay head-to-toe with Sam on the huge double bed; Jack was across the room, sprawled over cushions and beanbag.

Of course, I now understand why they encouraged me to agree to kill a dog. I crossed a line. If you can steel yourself to kill a pet, you might steel yourself to kill a person.

FOUR DAYS TO GO

✎ Draft Email

To:

Cc:

Subject: The Past

Someone else has to know the whole truth.

'Christmas Eve, 2016. The middle of London, next to Big Ben. Midday,' he said. Then I watched him disappear into the woodland. With anyone else, they'd be empty words.

It was so far in the future I thought we'd never get here.

I came close to telling you everything when we went to Compton for Gran's funeral. You mentioned the view from the houses in Compton across Lake Hintersea and how it must be full of memories. 'Yeah,' I said. Just *Yeah* – not *I can remember what we did as if it was yesterday.* Not *I can remember the faces of those who died.*

Someone else has to know the truth in case it all goes wrong.

I'm not sure when it all started to change. Maybe that night at the party. It was the first time I'd set out to hurt someone else.

Now you see why I have a dog, despite the hassle that Ewok is. And you understand why he had to be a Leavitt Bulldog.

I still have all the documents from the story – they're here in my bedroom in a small black metal case bound up with brown tape. You'll know it when you see it.

I can't believe |

Attachment

NOVEMBER 2011
BULLSEYE

I woke at 11.00 a.m. to find Sam and Jack gone, but heard a shout outside and stood in the window as they raced, neck and neck, up the steep zigzag drive and on to the gravel. They slowed as they passed the front door, bending over with exhaustion, and briefly touched hands. Sometimes I thought I could see tiny differences in their faces – Sam's thinner cheeks, Jack's heavier eyebrows – but from a distance, it was impossible to tell which was which. One of them looked up and beckoned me down.

They were having breakfast, reading magazines, when I arrived downstairs. 'Hi, Ben!' they chanted together. 'Toast?' As usual, their T-shirts had embroidered initials.

'I'm not sure that we should go ahead with what we discussed last night,' I said while aimlessly drawing circles with my knife. Breakfast, the bright sun, and the radio playing gently in the background had morphed Bullseye into a spirited, tail-wagging puppy.

'We certainly don't want to force you into anything,' said 'JT'. 'It's all for one, and one for all.'

'It's just . . . what if we're wrong – what if, after all, he's innocent?' I pushed my plate away, put my palms over my eyes, and groaned indecision as their father walked in.

'No one is really *innocent*,' Mr Thatcher said straight away. Even in daylight, he was the image of *Samuel John Thatcher, Ward of Hintersea*. He poured himself some coffee and leaned against the worktop. 'Given the right prompts, anyone can be corrupted.'

I think, in retrospect, that a glimmer of understanding passed between The Twins.

'Surely *you* don't know about this silly idea?' I glared at The Twins (who pulled faces that indicated regret). 'We were just . . . talking.' Their father was a lawyer – I was certain there was no way he would support what we had in mind. 'Look, I don't want us to get into trouble.'

'I know about *everything*.' He smiled at his sons and wandered off, coffee in hand.

Before I could say anything, my mobile vibrated in my pocket. 'HOME', read the display. 'Hi, Gran. Is everything OK?'

'Benny, when are you coming home? Something strange has arrived in the post.'

Panic detonated inside me. 'What sort of strange?'

The Twins stopped eating.

'It's a large parcel,' she said. 'I'm not sure what's inside.' There was a rustling sound. 'It's light, but fairly big.' Her voice was clipped. 'You should know that the postman had to ring the bell and I had to come all the way downstairs because you weren't here.'

'Are you sure it's for me?' I put the phone on speaker mode so The Twins could hear.

'Yes, it says "*Benny*" and "*private*" on the label. It's definitely for you.'

'Don't open it,' I yelled. 'It might, you know, be something personal.' I had to sound calm; otherwise, knowing what Gran was like, it would have the opposite effect. 'It might be from a girl, or someone messing around.' I knew I was talking rubbish. 'I'll be back soon; we're just leaving.'

'Well, I'll put it on the side for you. But I hope it isn't anything that you shouldn't be into.'

A few minutes later, I looked out of the car window in silence as Mr Thatcher sped us around the Lake. It was a sunny and unexpectedly warm day, and boats were out on Hintersea. I saw a couple of boys battling with a sail as we passed one of the landing areas at the bottom end of the Lake. Soon we passed Lakeside House and the sign announcing Compton Village opposite.

I invited Sam and Jack to come in, which meant painfully slow introductions with Gran as the package seemed to grow bigger and bigger. 'We're just going up to my room,' I said – words I hadn't used since Will died.

I ran my thumbnail along the tape and levered open the cardboard flaps.

It was packed with newspaper. *City at the Double: Manchester City 2, Stoke 0 and 25,000 flee as Mississippi floodgate opens* cascaded out: newspapers dated Sunday, 15 May 2011. I told The Twins that it was the same tabloid newspaper that I'd seen in Mike Haconby's hallway.

Then the hard black plastic of Will's cycling helmet. It had been missing since the day of his disappearance. I quickly withdrew my hands and gasped, 'Hold on. The police'll have to examine this.'

'Get a cloth or something,' said Sam. 'We need to see if there's anything else inside.'

I frantically rummaged around in the top drawer of my bedside cabinet and found a handkerchief. As I carefully pulled out the helmet by its strap, a slip of paper fluttered down:

TO BE PUT WITH THE REST OF MY THINGS.

It was Will's writing.

I started crying and shaking. Hyperventilating. Will really was speaking from the grave. 'I don't think I can go on. I think I need help.'

'Don't worry, Ben,' said one of The Twins. 'We're here with you.'

TO BE PUT WITH THE REST OF MY THINGS.

'What the hell?' I covered my mouth to stop my low groaning sound from being heard downstairs. 'Why? Why? Why? Why? Why?' I concentrated on making my chest rise and fall steadily. Then, somehow, I plucked out more newspaper – still the same tabloid from May 2011. The breathing I heard was my own.

Near the bottom, something solid, wrapped. I laid it on my bed and slowly unfolded the crumpled paper. Inside was a Dictaphone tape recorder.

I was overcome with dread and fear, unsure whether it held a message from Will or from his killer. Using the handkerchief, I laid the player on the bed and retreated slightly. 'I've got to know. Guys, I want you to stay, please.' Then I pressed PLAY.

After about three seconds, Will spoke in the slow way that people do when they know they're being recorded.

'Hi, Benny. It's Will. I hope you're cool. I've been given

permission to get this message to you. I'm not far away.' Pause.
'I'm going to be fine.'

There was nothing else, though we listened right to the end of the short tape.

'Run it back,' said Jack.

'. . . not far away.' Pause. *'I'm going to be fine.'*

'What?' I said, rubbing my eyes.

'Listen, after *not far away . . .'*

'. . . not far away.' Bark-bark-bark. *'I'm going to be fine.'*

It was faint, but it was there: *Bark-bark-bark.*

I played it again.

Bark-bark-bark.

And again, just that bit.

Bark-bark-bark.

With the sound up.

Bark-bark-bark.

I stood up and looked out of the window. Bullseye was trotting over the grass between Mike Haconby's front path and the caravan.

'We don't need the cops,' said Sam. 'We know who's behind this. Everyone in Cumbria knows.'

'The weirdo bastard. He's playing games with us,' added Jack.

I looked at the newspaper. It was definitely the same

newspaper I'd seen. Little things give people away, I thought.

I pulled down Will's Box from the top shelf of the wardrobe, put it on my bed, and opened the top. 'It's the box I told you about. You remember? The mementos. Bits and pieces that remind me of Will.' I held up an old *Solo Sail* key ring that was a present from Will.

Sam's mouth smiled – but, for once, his eyes didn't. He looked from Will's Box to the newly arrived items. 'I see you have quite a lot of Will's stuff.'

Jack whispered in my ear, but looked at his brother: 'We can do this, Ben. Let's complete this Challenge.'

Everything rested on the fact that it was Saturday, the evening that Mike went to the local pub. From what I'd heard, he just sat in a corner and drank a single pint, alone.

We had to cover our shoes. My gran had a large collection of plastic bags under the sink and I took six while running the tap noisily for glasses of water. That was my only part in the preparation.

We needed gloves. The Twins said that they had a packet of the plastic ones used for washing up.

The Twins would bring a stick about eighteen

inches long with a hooked end.

And they would supply a half-empty packet of rat poison. We would burn the container afterwards.

We weren't to buy anything suspicious; we wouldn't text about it; we would make only one telephone call. They returned home, and I spent the afternoon in a dreadful trance trying to write a History essay. My mood swung drastically: sometimes it felt obvious that Mike Haconby was responsible; at other times, the evidence seemed paper thin.

It was 9.30 p.m. when my gran said that she was tired and going up to bed.

'I'll stay down here and watch something,' I said. This wasn't unusual and meant she would expect the television to be on for a while.

At 9.55 p.m., I listened at the bottom of the stairs and heard the flush of the toilet. I slipped out the back door, which didn't have a Yale lock, so opened and closed much quieter than the front one, and tiptoed through the back garden. Just before I reached the road, I tied plastic bags round my shoes. If it came to it, the police wouldn't be able to find prints to match our trainers.

The bulb in my gran's room went off. There was a line of light between the curtains in our front room and, very faintly, I heard the start of the ten o'clock news. Otherwise, the houses on both sides were in silent darkness. Will's house had been empty for months. In the distance I could see the lantern-like room at the top of Lakeside House. Surely no one would be looking towards the village at this hour.

I hadn't heard The Twins arrive, and couldn't see them as I crept along the path that ran next to the oil-black lake. On this side of the houses, away from Compton Village's solitary street lamp, it was nearly impossible to see.

I heard fingers click as I shuffled into the garden. The Twins were on the lake side of an old shed.

They gave me no time to have final doubts. As soon as I arrived, there was a nod and we slunk towards Mike's bathroom window. The small one at the top was open for ventilation, and that meant Jack could lean through and open the larger bottom window with the hooked stick. Will's house had the same set-up, and I'd told The Twins we once had to break in when Will locked his keys inside. It's difficult to know when I passed the point of no return, but I suppose it was going through that window.

The house was filthy. My torch lit a brown shower curtain and bath tiles edged with mouldy black. The toilet was stained and the cork tiles at its base had peeled back. It smelt musty. Years of smoking had seeped into the fabric.

We came out into his hallway, next to Mike's blue bag of tools and opposite a small table. The telephone, the cord wrapped round it, sat on top.

'Be careful with that torch,' said Sam. 'You'll be seen from the road.'

The kitchen was also a mess. Blackened saucepans sat on the stove and the sink was full of plates and mugs. A glass of stagnant water sat on the windowsill, a couple of cigarette butts floating in it. In the corner there was a silver bowl with some scraps inside. The cupboard behind had an industrial-sized packet of dog food.

Jack used the top end of the stick to mix the poison into the bowl, and he added a handful of dog-food pellets.

I heard Sam creaking up the stairs.

'Sam, we've got to get going,' I hissed. 'Sometimes he's back before eleven.'

The floor above us squeaked as Sam moved across. Then Jack and I heard three solid knocks.

I followed Jack past the front door and up the stairs. Odds and ends were left everywhere: one stair had an old speaker, the next a plastic bag full of what looked like tins for recycling. The carpet was worn threadbare in the middle.

Upstairs, the room straight ahead was a bedroom. I flashed my torch inside: a single bed; clothes scattered over the floor.

'In here!' Sam spoke in the loudest whisper possible. 'Quick!' He was in the next room along, which was something like a spare room or box room – it was full of junk in plastic bags. At the time of Will's disappearance, the police had taken ages to go through everything meticulously.

Bills and papers, driving licence, chequebooks and the like, old and new, were scattered on a desk along one wall. But it was something else that had caught Sam's eye. He swore. 'I don't believe it.'

His little finger, gloved in pale yellow, pointed at a pad of notepaper. There was no doubt: it was exactly the same as the paper used for Will's notes. It was *exactly* the same – I even remembered a little dark speck in one corner that ran through all of the sheets. This wasn't just the same type of paper; it was the *very* same pad.

I was enraged. It wasn't a controlled, useful anger. I was a boiling whirlpool focused on revenge. Mike seemed weak and pathetic. Not really human. Scum. He was a bulbous-red-eyed killing machine; he was the sound of fingers scraping down a blackboard. He was the opposite of The Twins.

I couldn't think beyond how we'd been separated by only a thin strip of tarmac, how many times I'd wandered up his path, how many times we'd spoken, how many times we'd spoken *after Will died*.

'This man deserves more than a dead dog,' said Jack.

'Maybe we should wait here and confront him when he arrives?' I suggested. 'Three against one. We could do him in.' I imagined pushing and shoving, maybe some punching, then calling the police.

'No,' said Jack. 'He deserves *much* more.'

The Twins looked at one another and smiled.

NOVEMBER 2011
THE INCIDENT IN THE NIGHT-TIME

Sam glanced at his watch and started to walk downstairs. 'Let's go to the kitchen.'

I was worried he was going to suggest infecting Mike's food with rat poison, but that would have been very difficult, given that the only open packet I'd seen was sugar. Mike ate from tins.

It was Jack who went to the gas taps on the stove first. 'Thinking of these?'

Sam nodded. 'We might have half an hour. Let's leave these on and see if Mike does the job for us. If he lights a cigarette or turns on a light – it'll blow.' He looked at the four gas taps. 'We can turn on one each.'

'No,' I said, holding my hands to my chest. 'I think I've changed my mind. There's enough evidence for the police to be involved. We can have Mike rotting inside a prison until he dies.'

'Will Capling was your friend,' said Jack. 'You need to do this. It's a Challenge.'

'No. I don't think it's right,' I whined. 'I don't

care about Challenges.'

Their faces hardened.

'Come on. Guys?' I looked from Twin to Twin for support. There was one second when I thought that they were going to break into smiles. But I had jumped on to ice that I thought to be solid . . . and plunged through into arctic water. I couldn't understand the sudden change. These were The Twins – my heroes.

'I don't think it's right,' Jack mocked in a high-pitched voice. 'I don't think it's right to hurt the man who murdered my best friend. We should kiss his arse instead.' He wiggled from side to side, flopping his arms around.

'What?' My insides felt thin and watery. 'Why are you acting like this?' It was the first proper disagreement I'd ever had with The Twins.

'You don't really care about Will, do you?' said Sam, smoothly, the voice of reason. 'He never meant much to you. You probably don't give a shit about us either.'

'I don't like this. We can't *kill* someone. Can we?' Surely they understood? 'I don't want to do something I shouldn't.'

Jack laughed at me, then turned to his brother with intense seriousness. 'We're running out of time.'

Sam grabbed my face – he didn't hold hard, but it

would have been impossible to move. 'We've brought you this far and you can't change your mind now.' His hand moved to the side of my neck, still firm, but mock-friendly. 'We're special. We're supermen. We can do anything.'

Jack moved my arm so that my hand was on the tap. 'Come on. This man is *nothing* compared to us.'

Sam switched one. The gas hissed out.

Jack switched a second. 'Now you have to turn on one of those taps.'

It was only a gas tap. Just something that made the house smell; not much worse than blowing cigarette smoke around. We weren't shooting him or sticking a knife into him. I only had to twist a bit of plastic. Mike'd probably smell the gas, think he'd made a mistake, turn it off, and open the windows. What did it matter?

But this reasoning didn't really convince me. Deep inside, I knew this was attempted murder. OK? I KNEW IT. I HAVE TO SAY THAT. I KNEW IT. AND I HATE THAT I DID IT. But I was confused. Let's just face it: I made a mistake – and then it was impossible to go back and put right.

I switched one of the dials and more gas seeped into the room. Brain-paralysing fear spread into me.

One of The Twins, I'm not sure which, turned the

fourth. The room already smelt.

I rushed towards the bathroom window and then out into the garden; behind me, I heard the kitchen door close. I *nearly* raced back in and turned the gas taps off, but Jack and then Sam were clambering out of the bathroom window, and that meant I couldn't easily get back in. After some difficulty, the window was closed with the hooked stick.

We crouched in the garden behind the shed and Sam made us check that we had everything.

Jack quietly pressed his hand against Sam's. 'That was possibly our best-ever Challenge.'

'I'm absolutely shitting myself,' I said. Incomplete, pathetic, weak sentences spilt out of me. I ended with: '. . . don't want to do this.'

'You can go back in there if you want to,' said Sam. 'But we're not.' Neither Twin was going to move. 'You should go back to your house and pretend nothing has happened. If you say anything, you're on your own, because we weren't here.'

'*I* certainly wasn't here,' said Jack.

'And neither was I,' said Sam.

(I know that I still should have gone back into the house – I *do* get that.)

We crept down to the bottom of Mike's garden, which was only separated from the path along the river by a broken fence. Rocks pressed in the pit of my stomach. 'Where're your bikes?' I asked in a low, listless voice. Perhaps The Twins would notice how worried I was and take me back inside.

'We didn't come on bikes,' Jack said, nodding further down the bank of the river. 'We came by boat.'

Tied up next to the rowing boat at the bottom of Lakeside House was a small yacht: oars inside, outboard motor, sail tied to simple mast.

'I didn't know, I hadn't seen . . .' They hadn't mentioned sailing. I hadn't thought to ask.

The Twins smiled. 'You should get back to your house,' Sam said. 'It's dangerous round here.'

I ran through the field next to Will's empty house. The night seemed darker, the Lantern Room at the top of Lakeside House brighter. It was a long way away, but this wasn't a creation of my guilty conscience: there was definitely someone standing in the window.

I knelt in the living room and prayed that the gas would fail or Mike would smell it and open the window or something miraculous would happen to get me out of a terrible problem. I also prayed that I hadn't been seen. I should have smashed down the front door and explained everything to the police.

Instead, I sat watching the clock slowly tick.

Mike's van rumbled to a stop at 11.18 p.m. Shortly afterwards there was a bark from Bullseye and a slamming van door. The usual sounds.

The clock became intolerably loud.

Fifty-five minutes after we had turned on the gas taps, Mike Haconby entered, must have smelt the overpowering fumes, and instinctively switched on the light. That caused a tiny spark. That spark ignited the gas.

The ticking clock was replaced by an explosion that rattled the windows; next came the pitter-patter of fleck-like debris blown on to the glass by the breeze; finally, the dull roar of fire.

Upstairs, my gran's screams came out as desperate croaks. 'I'm dialling 999!' she shouted. 'Something terrible! An accident!'

'Yes, an accident,' I said to myself, numbly pulling back the living-room curtain. I imagined the scene from the middle of the Lake, supposing that was where The Twins were, in their boat.

'Benny! Go out and do something!' Gran shouted. I

heard her speaking to the emergency services.

The fire had yet to take hold on the road side of the house, and it was only when I ran out into the middle of the road that I realized Mike Haconby hadn't been incinerated by the fire, but propelled down his hallway towards his front door, which was about five paces down his path. All of the glass in his windows had been blown out, and rubbish from inside the house was strewn across his garden. Fire had already taken hold in the kitchen.

Mike's body was lying just inside the front door. Above him, smoke threaded its way towards the open air. My run slowed to a jog as I went up the path – it wasn't the fire that frightened me; I wanted to hope that he was still alive, just for a few more seconds. 'Are you OK?' I stupidly said as I knelt down next to him.

In films, when people die, it's really tidy – after the bullet, they hold the point of impact, look shocked for three seconds, then fall to the ground and lie still. But people don't really die like that. Mike's burned face is something I see when I close my eyes at night.

One of the lies I've told for over five years is that Mike was dead when I found him. But there was a bubble of blood that popped as he spoke: 'Why?' He winced.

'What?' I said, my hands shaking cut and blackened shoulders.

'Why?' It was little more than a push of air.

'You bastard!' My hands were squeezing. 'You did it, didn't you? You killed Will.'

'No.' One of his eyes was crusted shut, but the other widened. 'No. Promise.'

I waited for him to say more, but nothing came, and then I saw that his eye was lifeless and staring.

'Mike? Mike?' I shouted, pushing his chest in a hopeless, inept attempt at resuscitation. I dug my nails into my own chest, agonized, desperate, alone. Mike was gone: the gulf between life and death absolute; and yet just two hours ago, a thin sliver of time, tantalizingly small but totally impossible to bridge. If only I could go back two little hours . . .

My panic focused on myself – getting caught, being made to pay, feeling guilty. What if I'd left evidence behind? The police sometimes found tiny fibres or hairs that caught criminals. What if The Twins decided to tell? What if they lied and said it was all my fault?

The fire was beginning to spread down the hallway towards the front door; dark smoke was gathering and billowing. I coughed and the heat made my face tingle as I briefly looked up towards Mike's picture of Lake Hintersea. Behind the thin smoke, I saw the title at the bottom of the picture (it was actually a print, not the original, but I didn't know that): *Across Hintersea towards Timberline Lodge by M. W. Winter.* The view was from the Compton Village side of the Lake towards Cormorant Holm and the water beyond, with Timberline in the distance. I had no idea where the picture had come from.

My gran was in the road in dressing gown and slippers, moving as fast as she could towards me, screaming, unable to form words.

I grabbed Mike's arms and started to drag him away from the house and down the path. He was heavy, and I could only move him half a pace with each heave. The local newspaper later said that I was a hero for trying to give him dignity.

Bullseye, I found out later, had died instantly. Initially, I'd been worried about harming a dog, but on that night I never considered him once.

I managed to drag Mike about two-thirds towards the gate as my gran wailed. 'Another death in our tiny lovely village,' she said over and over, quieter and quieter, as she calmed.

After I placed Mike's arms by his side, I looked up

towards the Lantern Room of Lakeside House. There was someone there – a figure in the light. What if he had special binoculars to see in the dark? I was consumed by a dizzy, hand-shaking panic – a panic fuelled by the explosive thought of having to kill someone else to cover my evil tracks.

A few people arrived in this time: two cars were driving past, and the people in the house further north around the Lake. The couple in the first car tried to resuscitate Mike, but it was a swirling and bleak fifteen minutes before the paramedics and police arrived, then another five for the fire engines.

The fire had severely damaged the Hintersea side of Mike's property and had begun to creep into the roof space of the houses on either side, including Will's house. The road side wasn't charred, but black smudges hung against the walls, lit by the flashing lights of three fire engines, two police cars, the paramedics, and an ambulance. Hoses snaked past firemen standing in Mike's garden; water dampened down the house long after the flames had been defeated.

I was standing next to my gran in our front garden when The Twins arrived with their parents.

I saw Mr Thatcher talking to one of the policemen and

pointing towards me. He was still speaking when the PC brought them over. '. . . Seen clearly from the other side of the Lake,' was his final line, then he put his hand on my shoulder. 'Ben, I hope you're OK. We were watching TV together when Ann noticed the glow in the distance. The guys insisted that we come over and check you're OK.'

Sam and Jack were wide-eyed and terrifyingly convincing in their innocence. 'Hi, mate,' they said. 'Do you know what happened? We could see it from our house.'

'There was an explosion,' I said lamely. 'That's what I know.'

The Twins' mum looked at me sympathetically. 'Poor Ben. You've been through so much. You must be desperately churned up inside.'

'Yes,' I said.

She turned to the policeman and spoke quickly, though calmly. 'The boys and I came back from dropping a present off about – oh, the ten o'clock news started as we went up the drive – and we didn't spot anything then. What time did it happen?'

There was no way that she could have been with the Twins at ten o'clock, and the idea that they'd sat down together and watched TV was crazy; they weren't that sort of family, anyway.

'It was about eleven,' I muttered, looking at the passing fireman rather than her. 'I s'pose you were distracted by the television.' It just came out – I wanted to let them know I knew it was a pack of lies.

'Probably,' she said sweetly, as if indulging me. 'It's horrible to say, but there were a lot of explosions on the screen.' She turned to the policeman. 'We let the boys choose the film on a Saturday. I'm not a Bond fan.' Another smile at me. 'Anyway, is there anything that we can do?'

I shook my head. It hadn't occurred to me that The Twins would have their parents produce an alibi.

My gran went inside and Mr and Mrs Thatcher walked along the road with the policeman. I stood alone with The Twins and looked around to make sure we couldn't be overheard. The fire engines rumbled loudly and firemen called to one another.

'I wasn't expecting that,' I said, terrified that The Twins had made a mistake by letting their parents into the secret. 'What have you told them?'

'I don't know what you mean,' said Sam. 'We like a Bond film on a Saturday night. Very cosy.'

'Yeah? So which one was it?' I was losing myself in anger and desperation. Perhaps I should have showed them to be liars in front of the policeman.

'*A View to a Kill*,' said Jack, with a tiny snort of laughter.

Sam whispered in my ear. 'Or maybe *Live and Let Die*.'

I put my hands in front of my mouth to hide my words. 'Guys, I can't believe you're joking. We've killed someone. A person. A human being.'

'Don't think so,' said Jack.

'Not me,' said Sam.

The Twins' parents were striding up our garden path. 'Come on, boys,' said their father. 'The police want a word with Ben.'

Jack quickly, casually, glanced around to see if it was safe to speak. 'We're always looking to the next Challenge, Ben. The Games Master has something even more radical than this. Something you'll be fascinated to be part of.'

I was certain that the second half of what he said was heard by their parents. 'You need to go,' I said blandly. 'Thank you for coming over.'

Soon after midnight, I sat in my living room with my gran and a couple of police officers.

'Is there anything you can tell us, son?' said the man, who introduced himself as Toby.

'No,' I said. 'There was just . . .' And I started to cry.

'He's been through so much. He's such a good boy,' my

gran whispered, her eyes welling with tears.

Gently tapping me on the shoulder, the PC said, 'I think we can do this tomorrow at the station in Barrow.'

I saw a red light flashing on my phone and picked it up, as had become instinct after my friendship with The Twins. The text had been sent at the time that I was dragging Mike away from the fire.

> Sup on your side of the lake??
>
> Whatve U been doing??
>
> Hope youre OK

I looked at the policeman and at my phone. 'It's from friends,' I said.

'It's good that you've got support,' said the policeman.

NOVEMBER 2011
LONE SUSPECT

I spent Sunday afternoon at the police station in Barrow.

When I arrived, the reason was 'to be eliminated from their inquiries', which were proceeding because of the fear (confirmed later that week) that 'foul play was involved'. Mike had received anonymous death threats. I had been near the body and near the house and therefore might have contaminated the scene. They took hair and saliva samples and fingerprints. It was polite rather than friendly.

My gran stayed with me throughout – as I was under eighteen, it was my legal right to have an adult present. She sat with her hands pressed together, eyes to the floor, and didn't say anything other than greeting the police officers and thanking them afterwards. A feisty parent might have intervened more, I suppose.

The interview was in a beige-coloured room with a simple table and hard chairs. The interviewer, a sweaty man in a dark suit, spoke into a video camera on a tripod before he turned to me. 'We just want to establish what you know.' He sniffed. There was a female PC present, an emotionless smile stuck on her face.

The man started by asking questions about Saturday evening that were uncomfortably similar to the ones I'd been asked after Will disappeared. *Had I seen anyone? Heard anything? Any cars? Anyone in the road?* The focus changed to who I thought had committed the earlier crime, and whether I suspected Mike Haconby . . . *as everyone else did.* Near the end, some questions were more direct.

Do you think that Mike Haconby killed your friend Will Capling?

'No, not really.' I thought of the notepad and Bullseye's barking. 'I'm not sure. But it's not up to us to punish people.' *Us* – it just slipped out, not that they noticed. I wondered if it sounded too defensive. Perhaps if I got the blame for Mike's murder I would somehow be held responsible for Will's. I thought of my hand being guided towards the gas tap.

Did you go into the house over the road and leak gas for a joke?

The 'It was just a joke' defence. 'No. I was inside all evening watching TV.' It all sounded fake, as if I were detached from the words forced out of my mouth.

Did you have anything to do with the death of Mike Haconby?

I shook my head.

We need to hear you say it.

'No.'

The chairs made a low screaming sound against the floor as we pushed them back and stood up.

'Thank you for coming in,' the man said. 'We'll be in touch if we need anything else. Maybe later in the week.' His lack of a smile let me know it was not over. 'Don't leave the country, will you.' He snorted, his version of a chuckle, and took me through to write a statement.

Gran and I returned in a taxi in silence. I got out my phone. Ethan and Anna had been texting me daily, and there was one from her about the fire –

I hear theres been a fire
and you got a guy out

– and another about the following Friday's Sixth Form 'Christmas' Party. That party was renowned for being rowdy, and had moved from place to place over the years as venues refused to repeat the booking.

Cant believe our yr gets a hotel!!!
Hope youll be mageeek!

There was one from Sam, and one from Jack.

Jack:

> Hope it goes well with the cops. Just deny everything!!!!!
>
> The Gazette says you were in the action.

Sam:

> We're gonna rule at the party on Fri.
>
> Got the best ever challenge, youre gonna love it.

I read them both ten times, despairing.

After a silent tea back at home, I went upstairs, my head a jumble of hardened memories of Will and vivid pictures of Mike lying on his garden path. The moment I turned on the old stove's gas tap played like a two-second video clip.

In my room I dragged out Will's Box and poured the contents on to the bed. Spread out in front of me was his life as it had met with mine: his Rough Book, the *Solo Sail* key ring, a well-read lads' mag and loads of other bits and pieces: a little Yoda figure, a Carlisle United ticket stub, a twelve-inch wooden ruler with a microphone drawn at the top, a yo-yo . . . a lot else. Each item held memories. The things sent by 'Will' were also there.

I picked up Will's Rough Book. It was probably the only thing in the world that would bring a smile to my face. On the fifth page there was a drawing of our Headmaster, Mr Morris, as Spongebob. The pink blob next to him had '*Benny*' written above '~~Patrick~~'. A few pages later, there was a strange creation: half pop star, half muppet.

One picture Will got caught drawing was a band from *X Factor* . . .

But it wasn't there.

The whole page had gone.

Of course, the pages weren't numbered, but as I looked at the book more carefully, I realized that *six* pages were missing – and they *definitely* had been there . . . though I wasn't sure when I'd last seen them. I thought that they were parallel pages: when you remove a page from the front end you have to take one out at the back, or else it's really obvious that a page has been ripped out.

I was so stressed that my first thought was that I had somehow lost them. But that was stupid. They hadn't fallen out. They had been removed.

No one had been in my room on their own. I thought back to when The Twins and I planned the raid on Mike Haconby: no, I hadn't left them alone. Someone else had been in the house, crept into my room, and torn the pages out.

I thought about calling the police, but the last thing I wanted to do was encourage their attention. They would want to go through everything in the box, and it was none of their business. *The murderer secretly kept a lads' mag that belonged to his dead friend . . .* (Not that it was like that, but I knew how it would look.) I felt sick.

Someone had crept up the stairs, had touched Will's stuff . . . But why? What could possibly be of importance *now*? They had probably hoped I wouldn't look – and what were the chances that I would? I might have gone months or years – or forever – without noticing. That was why he (they? she?) hadn't stolen the entire book. As it was, I couldn't remember when I'd last seen the missing pages.

Nervous dread that The Twins were involved nibbled at me.

I hoped that I could work out what had been on the missing pages of Will's Rough Book by looking at the indentations on the page underneath, but this trick doesn't work nearly as well in real life as it does on TV. There were just squiggles and shapes – the best I could make out was a triangle with two words inside: *E*-something and *Cloud* (?).

The house suddenly felt insecure. If someone could walk

in when I wasn't there, they could walk in while I was asleep. Fears that had been controlled while I trusted The Twins came flooding back. I went downstairs and tried the back door: locked. And all the windows were closed (I was still thinking about The Twins).

'Are you OK? What are you mooching around for?' asked Gran.

'Just, um, checking,' I said. 'Does everything seem OK to you? Like, secure?'

'Benny, dear, please stop.' Gran smiled. 'Will you sit with me for a bit?' She turned off the television.

I sat in my usual chair, closed my eyes and breathed out deeply.

'Benny,' she started, 'I want to ask you something.'

This didn't sound good. I swallowed, then opened my eyes.

She leaned forward. 'You know that I'll love you whatever you've done.'

'I know.' But how would she cope with the truth? There was no way I could tell her.

'I need to know if you had anything to do with what happened to Mike. I need to know so that I can help you.' She laid her hands in her lap. I knew that she wouldn't say another word.

I picked my words carefully, still thinking of The Twins and how clever they were with answers. 'It wasn't me.' I looked her in the eye. 'It wasn't.' At least, it wasn't the *real* me.

'Thank you,' she said. 'I'm sorry I had to ask. I know that you couldn't do such a thing. Why don't we have a nice cup of tea?'

We watched a documentary called *The World at War*. Every dead body reminded me of Mike; every figure in authority reminded me of The Twins; the man with binoculars at the top of the observation tower on the submarine reminded me of Mr Winter in his Lantern Room.

I wasn't sure where my guilt ended and my fear of consequences started.

And there was something else, something that held my depression together: a vague sense that I was now a slave to The Twins, not even a servant, and certainly not a friend.

THREE DAYS TO GO

✏️ Draft Email

To:	
Cc:	
Subject:	The Past

Someone else has to know the whole truth.

'Christmas Eve, 2016. The middle of London, next to Big Ben. Midday,' he said. Then I watched him disappear into the woodland. With anyone else, they'd be empty words.

It was so far in the future I thought we'd never get here.

I came close to telling you everything when we went to Compton for Gran's funeral. You mentioned the view from the houses in Compton across Lake Hintersea and how it must be full of memories. 'Yeah,' I said. Just *Yeah* – not *I can remember what we did as if it was yesterday*. Not *I can remember the faces of those who died*.

Someone else has to know the truth in case it all goes wrong.

I'm not sure when it all started to change. Maybe that night at the party. It was the first time I'd set out to hurt someone else.

Now you see why I have a dog, despite the hassle that Ewok is. And you understand why he had to be a Leavitt Bulldog.

I still have all the documents from the story – they're here in my bedroom in a small black metal case bound up with brown tape. You'll know it when you see it.

I can't believe this is about me. Please read the whole thing before judging me. I want you to know all of it.

I know |

NOVEMBER 2011
BEYOND DEATH

You would think that the week that followed Mike's death was different, full of whispered conversations and frightened glances. You'd imagine that we were in huddles, ensuring our tracks were covered, warily checking over our shoulders. But it was as if nothing had happened.

I steered The Twins into an empty classroom on the Monday morning, after History. 'I'm going through hell, how're you guys?' I whispered.

'We're cool.' They shrugged. 'OK, no probs.'

'This is a nightmare!' I must have been wild-eyed. My head felt full of wool. 'What if the cops find something?'

'Like a knife with fingerprints on it?' whispered Jack.

'No, like, I don't know . . . something that fell out of our pockets.'

'Our pockets were empty,' said Sam. 'And I'm certain that you didn't drop anything.' He half smiled. 'Don't worry.'

'Come on, guys – surely you understand? I'm going crazy.'

171

'Look,' said Sam. 'We're the only people who know you did it. And we're not gonna tell anyone. You're our best buddy – you know that. You're a Challenger with us.'

'And we're sure you'll be up for the next Challenge,' said Jack.

'But I want to get out of this. I just want it to stop.'

'Stop?' said Sam. 'We're building up to the ultimate Challenge.'

'But – look . . .' I insisted. 'Please. This is not me, I don't want to be part of it.'

'We brought justice down on the man who killed your friend,' said Jack. He put his hand on my shoulder.

'We're bolted into this forever,' said Sam, his hand arriving on my other shoulder. 'We've trusted you more than anyone, ever.'

Their hands lingered on my shoulders and I felt them both press slightly, just as I'd imagine a parent would. For a second there was a tighter, more menacing squeeze. Then, together, they let go.

'And I think someone might have been in my room.' I hadn't planned to say anything. I suppose I half wanted their help, half wanted to see their reaction.

'You're kidding! What makes you think that?' asked

Sam. Either they were truly surprised, or they were amazing actors.

'Just a hunch,' I muttered. 'Maybe I'm wrong. I'm so tired and stressed.'

That break, The Twins played football as usual, living in the moment. I couldn't be bothered. It was one of the first really cold days of winter: the wind whistled down over Hadrian's Wall, but The Twins swaggered around with their sleeves folded back.

Anna and Ethan were late, so I called over to Blake as he walked past and we stood together, just as we used to, and I searched for something to say. 'Are you going to the Sixth Form party on Friday?'

'Might do,' he said.

I shivered and pulled my coat up around my ears. 'I think that I *have* to go. I'd like it if you were there.'

'Yeah,' he said, unconvinced. I'd dropped him after The Twins arrived and now he wasn't prepared to be picked up again.

Ethan crashed out of the school door and hurtled over. 'Hell! It's cold enough to freeze your balls off!' he started. Then a quick glance: 'Oh, hi, Blakey.'

Blake wasn't given time to answer.

'Now, Ben, man,' he carried on, oblivious to my

depression. 'One guess who Anna is talking to, nicely set up by Sam'n'Jack . . .' He held his palms out for an answer and then thrust them into his coat pocket. 'Bloody hell, why aren't we inside?'

Why *weren't* we inside? Because The Twins were outside.

'Anyway,' Ethan continued, 'she's talking to –' he made a trumpet sound – 'the sexy Caro-line! And she's trying to talk the poor gal into going to the party with –' trumpet sound again – 'Ben-the-love-machine!'

'Oh, good.' I was a wretched, ugly murderer – what was the point? Why bother?

'Don't look too excited.' He smiled. 'I reckon it can happen, man . . .' He lowered his voice. 'I heard Sam and Jack say that it was their number one Challenge to get you two together.'

I watched as Jack, ball at his feet, weaved past a couple of players, feigned a shot at goal, sending the keeper the wrong way, then trickled the ball gently into the other half of the net.

The week passed in a sleepless, aching haze. The longer it lasted without the police contacting me, the more obsessed I became with the idea that an arrest was imminent. But on Thursday, a police officer came to the house and explained to Gran that I 'was not part of their current inquiry'. I was, literally, going to get away with murder.

On Friday, the morning of the party, The Twins and I had a study period together in the school library. We had a regular place on a table at the far end between the Physics section and a window. No one else was nearby.

'All set for tonight?' asked Sam under his breath.

Caroline had agreed to go to the party with me 'as a friend'. Her relationship with Mark had faded since his embarrassment at the Halloween party, and he had started to go out with one of the girls who played football. I had been talking to Caroline in school and we had been to the same things a couple of times, but there was no suggestion that we were an item. I couldn't really claim that we were 'just good friends'. Caroline was still the girl against which all others were measured: I thought there was no one better looking or more fascinating – in fact, I wanted her to be slightly *less* beautiful so I could look at her without feeling awkward.

'I don't see how you can inspire Caroline to chase after someone like me,' I mumbled. 'There are some things even you can't manage.'

'There's nothing we can't do,' said Sam.

*

The party was going to be at the the Royal Northern Hotel in Grange-over-Sands – a venue that sounded much smarter than it was – and it was miles away from Wordsworth Academy, so the school was having to lay on transport.

I actually sat next to Caroline on one of the rickety double-deckers that pulled out from Wordsworth Academy at 6.30 p.m. We were downstairs. Anna and Ethan sat in front and turned around to talk to us most of the time. Apart from a draught from a window that wouldn't shut and general queasiness caused by the erratic motion of the bus (or perhaps from embarrassment when Caroline's leg touched mine), it was a journey happy enough for me to almost forget what had happened.

My eyes were occasionally drawn to Blake, sitting on the front left-hand seat nearest the driver, staring ahead, an empty place next to him. Every now and again an object flew forward in his general direction: a ball of scrunched-up paper, and then a coin, which narrowly missed him. Blake sat unmoved through it all.

The Twins were immediately behind me on the back seat, surrounded by other people from our Year.

The Royal Northern Hotel has now been converted into flats, but in 2011 it was on its last legs: brown patterned wallpaper, dirty beige curtains, a slightly sticky dance floor in a large stark room dominated by a huge disco ball – it didn't really matter if it was trashed.

Just before half past seven the buses pulled up across the road from the 'hotel' and everyone piled out, occupying the main road and running around on a bit of green next to the railway lines. The sea was an expanse of black beyond, lit only by the glow of the distant lights of Morecambe. An old couple were walking down the road, and three or four boys danced round them making stupid noises.

The Twins guided me towards some bushes at the far end of the green.

'How're you feeling?' asked Jack.

'A bit better.'

'Here's something to help you get through the evening,' said Sam. He made to shake my hand and I realized that something was being placed in my palm. It looked like a paracetamol packet.

'Guys, I'm not taking anything,' I said.

Jack whispered in my ear and kept one eye on the others as they started to make their way towards the hotel entrance. 'Hey, dude, all they do is help you *chill*.'

'There's no way I'm messing with my brain,' I insisted.

'Everyone's doin' it – they make you fly. It's what you

need,' said Jack. He gave me his innocent-looking smile. 'Come on, it's cold out here. Let's go in and *party*!'

I watched them run inside, then threw the packet of pills into the long grass next to the railway line. The metal tracks started to click and hum, then there was a fizzing and whirring sound: a train approaching from the left, its headlights glinting off the track. I stared at the driver.

Caroline was with the others inside. I was annoyed – I'd had this silly dream about walking in with her. 'I'm sorry, I was just – they . . .' I gestured helplessly. 'Never mind.'

There are so many stories that intertwine that evening, and mine is only one of them. The evening started with us all sitting around and laughing loudly at jokes that weren't really funny, then dancing self-consciously on a half-empty dance floor.

Given that I'd been offered those pills, I'm now sure that my drinks were spiked or drugged, and possibly Caroline's were too. I suppose it was part of The Twins' plan to get us together.

Just before the large 1930s-style clock showed nine, I'd been sitting at a table just inside the door with Caroline, not talking about anything in particular. The Twins had brought over more drinks and Sam said he knew we were getting on because we drank at exactly the same time, which apparently was a sure way to tell if two people fancy one another. Everything seemed simple, frivolous, funny. My worries turned to dust. The Twins seemed amazing – after all, they had never done anything to actually *hurt* me, and though some of what they did was radical, they seemed to have my best interests at heart.

The world slowly spun; everything was light. Caroline and I put our drinks down together and I remember moving my head towards hers. Suddenly we were kissing, a proper kiss, mouths open, eyes closed. I only pulled away when someone shouted '*Yeah!*' in my ear.

'Come on, let's dance again,' said Caroline, slightly glassy-eyed, and pulled me on to the dance floor.

Everyone was standing up for one of the most popular tracks. Our group started off dancing in a large circle – about ten of us, with Caroline next to me. Blake was the focus because he was completely hopeless and funny.

My arms and legs whirled round like a cartoon character's, and garbled nonsense spilt out of my mouth. I suppose I tried to compete to keep Caroline's interest, like a prancing animal trying to attract a mate. There was a clip of it on someone's phone: I look wild-eyed, limbs pumping in time to the music, circles of damp under my arms. At one point I pull Caroline close and kiss her on the neck. I didn't understand that something was wrong; I thought I was just hyper because of what had happened immediately before the song started – if I thought anything at all.

The circle broke down and Caroline started dancing with Blake; she held his hands and looked into his eyes. Everyone saw it as a bit of a joke – just Caroline being nice – and attention drifted away. A well-known song started and people sang loudly. There was so much going on; hundreds of sweaty people.

But I was consumed by the bubbling acid of jealousy. Because of Blake. Blake! Crazy. Caroline was just having fun. And Blake, for once in his life, was living the moment.

My mind was messed up and I would have done anything to make them stop. Why wasn't Caroline looking at me? Why wasn't she dancing with me? I felt she had toyed with me. Given the chance, I would have smashed the speakers and made the lights explode.

I stormed back to our table and glowered. Sam arrived with another fresh drink and I downed it in five gulps, never taking my eyes of the dance floor. All the normal pathways in my brain had been twisted.

The last thing I remember is Caroline and Blake dancing beneath a clock that showed the time as 9.25 p.m.

*

[Reconstructed from what Ethan told me weeks later]

I bumped into one or two dancers as I made straight for Caroline. One shoved me pretty hard, but undeterred I placed myself between Caroline and Blake and slurred things like, 'You need to dance with me now,' and, 'Here I am, what's going on?'

Blake was defensive and pleading. 'Come on, Ben, we're not hurting you, man.'

'This has got nothing to do with you,' I growled. I insulted his physical appearance and ridiculed his dancing.

People found this more interesting than the music.

'Just leave her alone,' Blake protested.

'Stay out of my way, or I'll kill you!' There were a hundred witnesses. I shoved Blake so hard that he stumbled back into a boy from the year above.

[Reconstructed from a phone recording]

After Blake was forced back towards me, things escalated: I held him in a headlock and shouted aggressive nonsense in his ear. As quickly as I grabbed him, I released him.

Blake, red-faced and dripping with sweat, ran towards the exit in his usual clumsy fashion.

I didn't bother to watch him go. 'Come on, just a little kiss,' I slurred to Caroline.

One or two people laughed; others shouted things at me. I ignored Anna, who thundered at me: 'Just piss off, you freak!'

The Twins ambled forward, smiling, feet tapping in time with the music.

I spun round to face them. 'This is all your fault. You made me do it.' Everything I said was at half-speed. 'You've taken things too far. I shouldn't have listened to you. No one would have got hurt.' I held my head in frustration. Everyone assumed I was talking about what had happened with Caroline.

But The Twins knew otherwise. 'Get him outside,' Sam snarled.

Ethan's tone, almost overlapping with Sam, was pleading: 'You need to go outside and calm down, man.'

Just before Sam and Jack reached me to throw me out (or knock me out), Caroline ran to the exit and I followed.

On the mobile recording, there follows a couple of seconds of Sam talking in Jack's ear. In that moment, I think they brought forward their plans against me.

We appear as slightly blurred, black-and white, silent-film figures, but there's no doubt it's Caroline and me, and no doubt what's going on.

She confronted me as soon as I arrived at the desk. Pointing and shouting, she obviously wanted me to come to my senses.

But the cogs in my brain just weren't connecting. I took half a step back, banging my palms against my head in sadness or desperation.

Given what later happened, Caroline made her best decision of the evening: she threw her hands up in frustration, brushed past me, and marched back into the party.

Almost immediately, Blake entered from outside. We had spent hundreds of hours together as friends and he surely expected me to have sobered up – but even the grainy tape shows that I was in a terrible state, twitching and twisting erratically.

Blake said something (I still don't know what).

I shouted and pointed with the spittle-flecked rage of someone who has lost their mind, then stepped towards

Blake and jabbed my fist at him.

He took two steps back, hesitated for a second, then ran.

And I dashed after him.

Four or five seconds later, Ethan, Sam and Jack appear and go outside to look for me. Ethan told me later that they searched up and down the road, but saw neither Blake nor me.

(There's four hours on the security tape after that. People come and go, and then, eventually, about 1.00 a.m., larger groups of people leave – but there is no sign of Blake or me.)

I have no memory of what happened after that, until just before 4.00 a.m., when I woke up next to the railway tracks.

I was some way round the corner from the hotel, back from the road, in bushes and gorse. My body ached and was as rigid as cold metal. The skin over my skull seemed to be drawn too tightly.

There was a cut about three inches long on my left arm, running down towards my wrist, and another on my left hand, roughly half the length of it. The cuts were sore, and red, and deeper than scratches, but they weren't bleeding.

I looked at my phone and saw ten unread messages,

all except one connected to what had happened with Caroline and Blake. The final one, timed at 1.43 a.m., was from Sam:

> We're back home. Hope you've made it up
> with Caro and sorted things with Blakey

That was by far the most positive. Anna's just said:

> bastard

Ethan's:

> that wasn't good man – where are you?

I sent one back to Sam:

> stuck in grange and don't know
> how the hell to get home

I moved my head from side to side and felt dizzy and sick. From somewhere nearby came a strange cacophony of cartoon noises: pings and tapping feet. Blake's ringtone. His phone was nearby.

'Blake?' I said towards the tracks. 'Are you OK, man?'

Nothing.

Using the torch on my phone, I fought through undergrowth towards the noise, which was coming from somewhere next to the barbed wire that protected the railway track. It was a neglected place: rusty lager cans and faded crisp packets caught by the thin fingers of the brambles.

After a pause, the ringtone started again and I saw the pale glimmer of Blake's phone three or four paces away, just within reach from my side of the barbed wire.

The caller ID flashed as *Mum&Dad*.

I held the phone up and away from me, as if it were a dangerous specimen, and called into the night air: 'Blake?' The phone kept pleading to be answered, vibrating desperately, but something kept me from swiping the bar to the right. When the noise stopped I saw that he had nine missed calls from the same number. I could see the start of a text:

Please call us, we're VERY . . .

There was no sign of Blake anywhere nearby. I searched for dropped clothing or flattened grass, but all I succeeded in doing was trampling the site, making it look as if something had actually happened there. 'Blake?' There was no sound except a car growling past.

I retraced my steps to where I'd woken up, then

lumbered to the road and round the corner towards the metallic cry of police radios. Blue lights swirled in front of the the Royal Northern Hotel.

Of course, there was no reason for me to hand in Blake's phone – I intended to return it to him along with apologies for being so stupid: not that I knew *how* stupid I'd been. As I wandered past the front of the hotel, hoping to find a bus stop, a policeman called over: 'If you're one of the Wordsworth lot, you need to get home right now. *Please.*' He waved his arm as if to scoop me along towards the main part of the town. 'The buses *finally* left two hours ago,' he huffed.

I stepped around someone's vomit. 'OK. Thanks.'

The front window of the hotel had been smashed and the manager was standing in front of it talking to another policeman. They shook their heads and gave me a tight-lipped look.

I trudged to the town centre to find that the first bus for Kendal was at 6.29 a.m., and that was only the first leg of the journey. I rested my head against the back of the bus shelter, unsure of how embarrassed and wretched I should be: at that time, I didn't know about anything that had occurred after 9.25 p.m.

The stars had been covered by clouds. As I sat at the

bus stop, drifting off into an uneasy, cold sleep at about 5.30 a.m., my phone pinged: *Ethan.*

> R u with Blake? He's not
> home & not on phone. His
> parents are doing their nut

I wrote back immediately:

> haven't seen him since last night

No sooner had I pressed SEND than Blake's phone rang again. *Mum&Dad* for the tenth time.

I knew I was going to return Blake's phone, so it would have been weird if I hadn't answered.

I didn't have time to speak before his mum did. 'Oh, thank God you're well, we've been worried sick. We said that going to that party was a bad idea.' The words came out in a relieved tumble.

I wasn't sure what to say and made a sort of stupid dull clicking noise.

'Blake, dear? Darling? Blake?' Her switch to panic was immediate.

'It's not Blake,' I mumbled. 'It's Ben, his friend. I picked up his phone.'

'Where's Blake? He's never been out this late before, you know. Never.'

'I don't know. I just found his phone and was going to give it back to him.' It made me sound like a passer-by.

'Where did you get his phone from?'

I pictured the place next to the railway tracks. 'I found it, um, in some grass.'

'Oh my God, oh my God! This is terrible. Where is Blake? We need to speak to the police. Who did you say you were?'

'I'm Ben.'

Breathless and desperate words: 'Oh my God. I thought you were his friend. You're the boy he was fighting with. What have you done to him? Where did you last see him?'

'I don't know.' And then I turned the phone off. I wanted it all to go away.

NOVEMBER 2011
PUPPET ON A STRING

It was about half an hour later that a police car pulled up in front of the bus stop and a policeman spoke from the passenger window. 'Can we help you, son? What's your name?'

When I murmured the truth, he was out of the car immediately.

'We're looking for a boy called Blake Coldwell,' he said. I knew it was more of a question than a statement.

'*Caud*well,' I said (stupidly). 'Yes, I know he's not home yet.' I pulled his mobile phone from my pocket. 'I've spoken to his parents on this. I found it.'

'Do you know where he is?' he asked. 'His parents have said that he's missing, and that's seriously out of character.'

'No – I must have, er, fallen asleep somehow . . .' I must have looked guilty; I certainly felt guilty, though I wasn't sure why.

'How'd you get his phone, Ben?' It was strange to hear the policeman use my name. Perhaps it's a technique they're taught; perhaps it was meant to be friendly. To me, it was a sledgehammer blow.

'I found it in some grass near to the hotel. I heard it ringing.'

'Just passing by, were you?'

'No.' I looked down at the ground. 'I just woke up there and heard it.'

The other policeman had also left the car. 'Bit of a cold night to sleep out, eh?'

'Could you show us where you found the phone? Then I think we'd like to talk with you properly, down at the station. OK? Who should you tell?'

They listened as I called my gran and asked her to get a taxi as soon as she could to the small police station in Grange-over-Sands. Her high-pitched voice wavered at the end.

Four more police officers surrounded me at the station, energized by the frantic worry of Blake's parents. His mum and dad were insistent that Blake would never, ever, not in a million years, stay out all night – and in any case, everyone knew that Blake had not returned on the official buses.

I had his phone.

Worst of all, hanging over me like the darkest and most hideous of clouds, was the thought that I had done something to Blake that I couldn't remember. I vaguely remembered being irrationally angry with him. If his body was found a little way down the railway tracks . . .

The police certainly saw the same logic. It's normally a while before a missing-person inquiry reaches the stage this one did, but the Cumbrian Constabulary had people searching along the Grange-over-Sands seafront on Saturday morning. This was even before the mention of 'Blake Caudwell's disappearance' had hit the news.

The police were methodical. They searched half a mile in either direction of the Royal Northern Hotel, between road and sea, and every garden on the other side of the road for the same distance.

Later on the Saturday, when it was obvious to others, as well as his parents, that Blake had actually gone missing, a forensic team examined the area where I'd found his mobile phone. I had trampled the area so much that it looked like several people had been there – but they found nothing: no fibres on the barbed wire, nothing on the brambles, no sign of a struggle. And yet his mobile phone had been there. It was as if he had walked to the edge of the barbed wire next to the railway tracks and disappeared into thin air.

Except that wasn't the obvious explanation. They were circling me, hungry for my guilt – the obsessed magician who'd kissed his dream girl and then seen red when she danced with another boy.

They took my fingerprints and a DNA swab from my cheek, exactly as they had when I was taken in after Mike's death. I didn't mention that.

I sat in an empty cell and wasn't interviewed until late on the Saturday. I think that's because they were waiting to see what they found. Every time the outer door opened, or the hatch of my door slid back, I thought they were going to tell me that Blake's bloodied remains had been discovered.

It was then only a matter of time before they started to reconsider Will's death.

And Mike's.

When they interviewed me, I sensed a confidence that it wouldn't be long before they discovered an ugly truth – or truths.

The interview started at about 5.30 p.m. on the Saturday.

My gran sat on a blue plastic chair to my right, and there were two police officers opposite. The man, who introduced himself as Detective Inspector Leslie, did all of the talking.

I pulled down my sleeve to hide the cuts on my arm and hand.

After formalities came the ominous words of a caution: 'You do not have to say anything. But it may harm your defence if you do not mention when questioned something which you later rely on in court.' He coughed. 'Anything you do say may be given in evidence.'

I nodded. 'Yes.'

'So, is there anything you would like to tell us?'

I didn't say anything, but the room wasn't silent. I could hear the steady tick of the clock and the gurgling of a radiator. There were raised voices outside.

'It'll be easier if you tell us straight away what has happened to Blake.' DI Leslie leaned forward. 'We know that you were angry with him and threatened to kill him. Tell us how you see it.'

Two words – 'I don't . . .' – escaped from me before the door opened and Mr Thatcher swept in and relaxed into a chair next to me.

DI Leslie listened to some whispered words from a younger policeman who had followed in Mr Thatcher's wake.

'Will you be charging this boy?' Mr Thatcher asked, his hands resting casually on the table in front of him.

He had no notes, no jacket, no tie.

'That depends on the outcome of this interview,' said DI Leslie.

'I thought it might depend on the production of actual evidence.'

DI Leslie: 'We have a missing boy!'

'That,' said Mr Thatcher, 'is the *absence* of evidence. And the absence of evidence will enable my client to walk out of here – either now, or in –' he glanced at his watch – 'about twenty hours.' Mr Thatcher paused for about five ticks of the clock. 'But the compensation we will claim for wrongful arrest will rise with each passing second.'

'Hold on,' spluttered DI Leslie. 'He came in with the missing boy's phone.'

'Oh – arrested for theft, is he?'

'And you know full bloody well he was seen arguing with him earlier in the evening.'

Mr Thatcher raised his eyebrows. 'So you are charging him for breach of the peace? Who made the complaint?'

DI Leslie swore. 'You know that this is ridiculous!'

'You need to stay calm, Detective Constable.' There was a slight pause. 'Sorry, I mean Detective *Inspector*.' Mr Thatcher wore a resigned look. 'You must be aware of the irregularities in this arrest. I would like to bet that the police didn't identify themselves as such, nor did they tell my client he was under arrest. All *highly* irregular. And my client is under seventeen: his arrest must be unavoidable, not just because he had a few cross words with a classmate who has done a runner.'

DI Leslie couldn't bear to look at Mr Thatcher. He thumped the table. 'OK. Get the boy out. But I want to know where he will be – and if I find one speck of him or his clothing anywhere near a crime scene, he'll be back.'

Outside, I slipped into the back seat of Mr Thatcher's Mercedes next to my gran. Mr Thatcher looked at me in his rear-view mirror. 'Thank you,' I said.

'It's not a problem,' Mr Thatcher replied. 'I know that you didn't have anything to do with the boy's disappearance.'

My gran squeezed my arm. It was comforting to know that people were on my side.

Mr Thatcher continued: 'And it wasn't in anyone's best interests for you to be dragged into talking about things the police need not know.'

Mr Thatcher dropped Gran and me at home on his way back to Timberline. We stood in the road as the lights of the Mercedes disappeared down the lane. Above them, above the trees, I saw the Lantern Room at the top of

Lakeside House, lit as always, overseeing the village.

'I'm tired,' said Gran. 'Let's eat. You can tell me what I need to know.'

I missed out all the bits of the story that illuminated the central horrible truth: that I had flown into The Twins' web. In fact, I didn't mention The Twins at all.

'I had an argument with a friend and now he's missing. He's probably run off somewhere,' I concluded. 'Gran, it's as simple as that.' If only. I was still haunted by the thought that I had done something.

Upstairs, something drew me to look at Will's Rough Book.

But something had been added to the box: a plastic bag. And half sliding out of it was a pale blue coat.

It was like falling down a hole, only to find that you haven't reached the bottom – that the ledge you're on is creaking and snapping and then you're falling and falling again until *THUD* – you smack against solid concrete.

It was the coat Blake had worn to the party.

I dashed to the window and closed the curtains, catching a glimpse of the Lantern Room of Lakeside House lit up down the road. But Mr Winter couldn't look directly into my room from there – the angle was wrong.

I held the coat up and a Wordsworth Academy ID card

fluttered on to my bed, face down. I flicked it over with a fingernail, gingerly, trying to avoid contamination or fingerprints. As I feared, there was a picture and a name: *Blake Caudwell.*

Then my attention was back on the coat and two red blotchy smudges near the top. Blood. I looked at the cuts on my left arm and wrist. The pattern and length matched. It was *my* blood.

I breathed deeply – in and out; in and out – my shoulders rising and falling in exaggerated fashion. I felt claustrophobic. Totally alone. Beyond crying.

I had to be logical. I retreated into a corner of my brain, away from emotion, away from myself.

It was my blood. Not Blake's. I hadn't been home after the party, so I couldn't be a psycho killer without knowing it. It was impossible that I had somehow had the coat with me all the time – the police would have seen it. It *couldn't* have been me.

But who else would believe that?

My phone pinged.

Sam:

Hi Ben. Hope you're not finding this too much of a challenge . . .

NOVEMBER 2011
THE LANTERN ROOM

I know you'll think I should have gone to the police. The thought did cross my mind, but it wasn't *just* that I would have turned up with the bloodied coat of a missing person – think what they would have made of *that* – but also that I was terrified of being caught for what *actually* happened to Mike only a week before.

I felt like a puppet dangling on The Twins' strings. If I did go to the police, I was certain Mr Thatcher would ensure I was found guilty of *at least* one murder.

I could and *should* have gone to pieces. But there was a hard pebble of determination that resisted everything and everyone, including The Twins. Perhaps it was born out of my fury at what had happened to Will and what was now happening to me. I had to take control. It's what Will would have done. It's what The Twins had done.

The first part of every magic act is to convince the audience that everything is as they expect it to be.

I sent a text back to Sam:

The Twins, supposing it was them, could tip off the police at any moment – what if their Challenge was to get me into prison for as long as possible?

I had to hide the coat, but not in the usual places (sock drawer, under the mattress, behind a picture frame), nor in the creepy locations I imagined a murderer would use: in the shed or greenhouse, under a floorboard. I shouted: 'Gran, can I use your nail scissors for a sec?' It was the blandest reason I could think of for going into her room. A magician knows never to make a move furtively if you can make it openly.

'Yes. That's fine, dear,' she called back from the bottom of the stairs.

I moved quickly as her steps came closer. I took one of her old winter coats off the hanger, hung Blake's coat on it, then slipped my gran's back over the top, and put both of them in the wardrobe.

Her voice came from nearby. 'Have you found them?'

I coughed and clicked her wardrobe shut an instant before she turned the corner into her room. When she came in, she found me nibbling away at the nail on my

200

left thumb. 'It's strange that this was annoying me, despite everything else going on,' I muttered.

Once I knew that Gran was asleep, I went into the kitchen to get myself a glass of water. While the tap was running, I took a cardboard packet of frozen cod from the freezer. Then, quietly, quickly, I taped Blake's identity card to the inside of the packet and put the fish back inside. With the tap running a second time, I put the packet to the back of the freezer, behind a bag of peas.

The letters from 'Will'? I really wanted to keep these in my bedroom, but this was exactly the thought I had to fight.

I listened for noises from my gran's room – nothing – then tiptoed to the cupboard under the stairs. At the back, behind a rainbow-coloured feather duster and a plastic broom, was an old vacuum cleaner, now replaced by a newer model. I eased off the front plastic cover and a thin cloud of dust mushroomed into the air as I pulled out the bag used to collect the fluff. I then dropped Will's letters into the bag and replaced everything.

Perhaps I *had* gone mad. I'd never been *this* methodical.

Upstairs: silence.

In the drawer in the sitting room were my granddad's

binoculars. They were old and heavy, but magnified everything amazingly.

I turned off the kitchen light and crept into the back garden. In my dark clothes it would have been difficult to see me – inside the shed, I was surely invisible. I cleared cobwebs and mouldy grime off the window and looked behind the houses and above the trees: there was a clear line of sight to the Lantern Room of Lakeside House, about half a mile away. It was 11.15 p.m. but their light was still on.

Why the hell was someone up there at this hour?

I tried to focus on the room at the top of the old house. Even resting my elbows on an old lawnmower, the magnified circle wobbled and vibrated. But if I squinted, I could make out a smudge that was surely a person.

Suddenly, the Lantern light went out. As if it made any difference, I held my breath. Perhaps it was because a car was coming down the lane, lights on full beam, illuminating the trees and faintly throwing a grey tinge on Lakeside House.

For a second, I thought I saw a glint in the window. Maybe I imagined it, my brain convincing me that someone was up there, looking back at me, binocular to binocular.

I was certain Mr Winter was my best chance of confirmation that someone had broken into our house.

Worries and ideas bounced around inside my head that night after I returned to my room. I slipped into sleep a few times but woke at the slightest noise.

About 6.30 a.m., there was the ping of a text.

Jack:

It'd be good to see you this morn

The police had suggested that I stayed in Compton for a few days: they said it was because the situation was 'confused' and 'people wouldn't understand'. They wanted to know exactly where I was, 'just in case you're needed for inquiries'. But they didn't say that I couldn't meet with people.

I sent a text back:

Time?

Jack:

9

Me:

Where?

Jack:

> C u by the church

Where Will had been found.

After breakfast, I told my gran that I was going 'out for some air'.

'Don't be long,' she said from the kitchen at the back of the house. 'The police said that they would call back again at lunchtime.'

It was an overcast, windy day, and a few leaves swirled in the air as I took the route that Will had on the day that he died. Yellow and black *Do Not Cross* tape flapped in front of Mike Haconby's empty house. The graveyard and church stared back, cold and stonily silent.

I looked up to the Lantern Room and there was Mr Winter, a distinct shape behind the greyness of the glass. My witness.

The Twins didn't arrive on bikes as I expected. I was slightly early, so wandered through the graveyard, past weather-beaten flowers and a small wooden cross that had tilted sideways at a forty-five-degree angle, and saw the boat cutting across the Lake, driven on by strong winds. It could have been Will, back from the dead, but then I saw the two people on board.

'Hi, Sam. Hi, Jack,' I said, as loudly as possible as they neared the shore.

'Hiya, Ben.' I couldn't tell them apart. I think it was Sam.

Then I saw the name on the boat. *Evening Cloud*. I thought back to Will's Rough Book and how I couldn't make sense of the imprint of the triangle with two words inside: *E*-something and *Cloud* (?). Now I realized it was a sketch of The Twins' boat, *Evening Cloud*.

It was the first time I had the upper hand. I turned to face Lakeside House, pulled out my phone and quickly switched it to record. Then I waved at the Lantern Room.

The figure behind the glass raised a hand in acknowledgement.

When I turned, The Twins were dragging the boat on to the gravel at exactly the spot where Will's body had been found. I spoke quietly and calmly: 'You knew Will, didn't you? You sailed with him. You were friends with him. And Will kept it all from me.'

The Twins immediately stopped and looked at one another. The wind blew the rope of the church's flagpole against the metal. It whipped and chimed for ten seconds. The Twins both looked at me, silently, as if they needed time to communicate telepathically.

I nudged my phone nearer the top of my pocket so that the microphone would pick up anything said.

'Come in the boat with us,' said Sam.

I looked at the restless water, frothy with wind. 'I'm not keen.'

'It'd be good for us to be out in the open,' said Sam (let's suppose I had them the right way round). 'Nowhere to hide. No secrets.'

'We have things to tell you,' said Jack.

'I'm not sure,' I said. 'A lot has happened. Too much.'

Sam nodded. 'Why don't you get aboard,' he said. 'And we will tell you *everything*.'

I looked at the brooding Lake Hintersea, then back at the Lantern Room of Lakeside House. Mr Winter waved, three times – and I waved back.

The Twins saw. *I have you now*, I thought. *You will not be able send me over the edge.* I shrugged away Sam's help and clambered in, feeling like one of those crazy kids in a horror movie who put themselves in danger instead of running away. But where would I run to?

We pushed off from the edge and I felt the unsettling, insecure confusion of sloshing water. The boat sank and rose. The Lake was like The Twins – unpredictable, powerful, deep.

We didn't speak until we were a couple of hundred yards from the edge.

'You were with Will last Easter, weren't you?' I said. I had to take them through it logically. My hand rested against my phone.

Sam held out his hand and wiggled his fingers as if beckoning me. For a second I thought he was asking me to stand up. 'Your phone,' he said.

'Why?' I swore. 'You can use your own.'

'If you don't hand over your phone, you'll never *know*,' said Jack. 'It will always be a mystery – like a magician's trick.' He clicked his fingers.

I pulled it out of my pocket and it made a couple of quick pinging sounds as I pressed the red button. I had nine minutes of recording.

Sam's hand sprang out and grabbed it before I could stop him. 'You won't need this any more.' And he dropped my phone into Lake Hintersea.

My hand trailed in the water in a pathetic attempt to retrieve it. 'You bastard!' I said. 'You complete bastard!' I looked over the edge, trying to get a sense of our position, wondering if a diver could find something the size of a phone – and even if he did, whether it would actually prove anything.

'You should be more trusting,' said Sam. 'I thought you were a Challenger with us.'

I told them where they could stick that idea.

'You know who painted this boat with us?' said Jack.

I looked away. There were a couple of other boats on the lake, but they were too far away to help. But, as always, we were within sight of the Lantern Room of Lakeside House.

'There's actually only one piece of evidence that Will was our good friend,' said Sam. He pointed at three initials to the right of his seat: *WC, ST, JT*. Will, Sam, Jack. 'Scratched after we painted it. A mistake. We haven't made mistakes since.' Sam worked at the *WC* with the end of his key. The *W* became a set of hatched squiggles; the *C* became a distorted circle.

'You're going to prison for a very long time,' I said.

'I think *not*,' said Jack. 'Our family has been playing what you might call "Games" for generations. In any case, Will just sort of *happened*. The plan was for Will to go missing for forty-eight hours, that old Challenge, which he *agreed* to, even to the point of writing the letters we dictated, and then he started to think it wasn't such a good idea. And then we . . .' Jack looked away as if he was remembering the series of events. 'And then he slipped.' He stared me in the eye.

It was the matter-of-fact-ness that terrified me. 'What?' Desperate, fearful, I looked back to the shore. 'I want you to take me back. I have to check in with the police at lunchtime, you know.'

Sam pulled in the sail and we bobbed around the water, rotating very slowly. 'Let's not forget,' he said, almost to himself, 'that you killed Mike Haconby and, it certainly *looks* like, Blake Caudwell – whose body is still to be found . . .'

'Probably to be found,' added Jack. 'Or he might –' he clicked his fingers again – 'reappear! Like a card from a magician's sleeve.'

I wrapped a tuft of hair round my finger and pulled in desperation. 'You're both completely mad.' I looked at the acres of water. I was out of my depth with The Twins. 'I don't know what to do,' I said, my eyes welling up. 'I just want you to take me back to Compton.'

'Look, Ben,' said Sam. 'You know that we operate to higher principles. We can't break the rules of the game. The rules are set by the Games Master – and he's following the rules of the previous Games Master, back through our family for generations. You're still very much part of our Challenge. We need you as much as you need us.'

I hoped that Mr Winter was still watching. I needed

him to see us – I needed him to see this boat. Maybe he took photos.

'What must I do now?' I said. I hadn't given up, but I had to regroup – to think.

Sam leaned forward as Jack started an outboard motor to take us back to the shore. 'I promise you that we will *never* hurt you. You would hurt yourself before we hurt you. You're part of our world now.'

Jack put his hand out but I shied away. 'A promise from him is a promise from me,' he said.

I nudged baked beans around my plate at lunch.

'Nothing lasts for ever,' my gran said.

'I *know*,' I mumbled.

The knowledge of knowing who had killed Will was hollow. I didn't really feel sadness – it was more like despair.

I wished I had taken a second recording device or tipped the police off in advance. Now all I could claim was that they had destroyed my mobile phone.

To go to the police before getting evidence from Mr Winter would throw me into a battle I'd lose against The Twins and their dad. And Blake's coat was upstairs – I was a suspect in Mike's death. I shivered.

The house phone rang.

'Hello,' my gran said. 'Yes he is . . . But that doesn't mean he's dead, does it? There's still hope for the boy . . . Yes, Ben's depressed, the poor lad . . . Just for some fresh air . . . No, I promise he won't leave the village . . . Thank you . . . Thank you . . . Yes, thank you.'

My gran explained that there was still no news of Blake.

I pushed the beans around again, hoping I was clever enough to get myself out of this.

'I don't want to sit around in the house,' I said. 'I'm going out for another walk. I need to keep my head clear.'

'You won't leave the village, will you?' my gran said.

Don't leave town. It sounded like something from a cop show. The police didn't have a court order. I could do what I liked.

I didn't want to tell her about visiting Lakeside House: it was too wrapped up in a complicated story. 'I won't go far.' It wasn't a lie.

'You'll take your phone with you?'

'Yes, OK.' The lie slid out easily.

I put on my jacket and trudged down the road, seen by only one person: Mr Winter, the watcher at the top of Lakeside House.

The driveway, even under trees that had shed their green, was damp and dreary. The trees above clicked their branches together as if they were impatient fingers. A wave of hopeless depression washed through me. Everything that The Twins had said rang in my ears.

Mr Winter was a mystery to me, but I was sure that his wife would help. She was weird, but she wasn't awkward. If anything, she seemed to be the sort of person who would take my wacky logic seriously.

I gave a pile of leaves a kick, and as they settled I looked up and Mrs Winter was there. With papery skin under heavy make-up, she looked old. But her green eyes sparkled and she smiled energetically and widely, revealing gravestone-grey teeth.

'Mrs Winter, I wonder if you could help me,' I said, failing to smile.

'I thought it was you leaving footprints in the road. My *daaaahling* boy, of course I will help.' She stepped back and opened the door. 'Please come in out of the whirling wind.'

The door clunked shut behind me.

The floor was tiled and the walls wood-panelled: it was dark despite three candle-like bulbs flickering high above me. There was a large picture of Lake Hintersea looking towards Lakeside House and Cormorant Holm, more or less the view from Timberline.

Mrs Winter saw me looking. 'One of mine,' she said. 'Not that all of mine are landscapes. Not at *all*.'

There were four portraits hanging in the hall. 'They're very good,' I said.

'Thank you. They're just half-remembered faces.' She shuffled on and we came into a large sitting room. 'Would you like tea here, in the drawing room?'

'Well, yeah, OK,' I said, nervously perching on a stiff sofa.

The room was dominated by a very large painting that included most of the lake. I saw the title at the bottom: *The Wardship of Hintersea*. This was the view from Ward's Fell – Lakeside House in the foreground, then the lake, and on the opposite side, roughly in the middle, Timberline, surrounded by trees.

I stood up and had a closer look while she left the room. It was a picture that captured all the scenes of my life. There were even boats on the lake. I liked the idea that one of them could be Will.

'I am very proud of that one,' Mrs Winter said, returning with a tray carrying a teapot. 'I painted that soon after I came here. I was up on the mountain.'

'How long ago was that?' I asked. 'Um, if that's not a rude question.'

'1971. And in case you wonder, my darling, I was twenty-two. Forty wonderful years ago.'

I shifted uncomfortably in my seat. 'It was Mr Winter I was hoping to see, actually. I sometimes see him up in the Lantern Room.'

Mrs Winter cackled. 'My darling, darling sweet boy. My name is Winter, not his. I'm Miss Winter, really.' She leaned forward conspiratorially. 'We're not married, but I know that's what many people think.'

'Well,' I mumbled, shrugging, giggling a little in embarrassment rather than amusement. 'Lots of people don't get married these days.'

She laughed again, longer and louder. 'My sweet darling. What they say about you is true.'

I forced myself to chuckle politely, but didn't get the joke. 'I just want a quick word with him. He may have seen something important.'

'Everything looks brighter after a nice cup of tea,' Miss Winter said as she poured from a flower-patterned tea pot. 'Biscuit?'

I was impatient to get upstairs to see the man I thought was Mr Winter, but there was no point forcing her. She

214

was probably lonely. It was like a magic trick: be patient; go at the speed that draws your audience in.

'So,' I said, searching for conversation. 'Do you still paint?'

'Sometimes. The occasional landscape. Some large modern pieces. Sometimes the family of the Master of the House,' she said. Miss Winter looked out towards the lake. 'I adore painting his beautiful darling nephews. And his son.'

There were no pictures of boys or girls in this room, unless they were the figures in the painting next to the French windows that overlooked the garden: the painting of a boat cutting across Lake Hintersea. At the top of the stairs to my left I could see a more modern piece, made of swirling colours and patterns. 'Is that also yours?'

'Yes,' she smiled. 'More tea?'

I quickly finished what I had and held out my cup.

'Does your grandmother know that you're here?' Miss Winter asked.

'Not exactly.'

'She probably thinks you're up on Ward's Fell . . .'

'Yes.' I wriggled about on the hard sofa. I didn't feel right.

'Right, my darling.' Miss Winter stood up and held

215

out her hand. 'Why don't we go up to the Lantern Room? I'm afraid he can't come down, you see. His mind won't let him. That's his whole world up there – looking at the village and the Lake, seeing what happens, studying every detail. Master of it.'

'That's just what I was hoping for,' I said. 'Do you really think he sees everything?'

'Oh, my darling, he sees absolutely everything and is in charge of it all.'

Miss Winter took my arm as I stumbled up the first few stairs.

'Yes, it's his whole world. He is the unseen hand pulling the strings. The Master of it all.'

But my mind was on the modern painting. It was extraordinary, spreading up the wall and on to the ceiling. It must have been twelve feet by six, a swirly sky above a mountain, lopsided houses at the bottom. Vaguely Van Gogh in style. *Vaguely Van Gogh in style.*

I couldn't work it out. I had seen something very similar before. In The Twins' house? I couldn't focus.

We went up two more staircases. I didn't look at anything apart from the stairs in front of me. Blue carpet and then red. Step after step. Unthinking. And then there was a final flight to the Lantern Room. The stairs were narrower here, and wooden. I could see the detail but didn't understand what was going on around me. The stairs were dark wood with the swirly imprints of tree rings.

'I don't think I want to go up there,' I said. It was difficult to focus outside a thin strip of clear vision. There was a hissing and gurgling in my ears. 'I want to go home. Please.'

'Answers are at the top of those stairs,' she whispered in my ear.

My head was spinning.

I thought it was The Twins. The Twins said it was The Twins. But now I know it's you. I don't know if I said it aloud.

'You go ahead of me,' Miss Winter said.

I couldn't stop my legs. *Thud, thud, thud* as I ascended.

At the top there were windows looking in all directions. I thought that the room was filled with bees or flies, but these were the dark splotches that precede unconsciousness.

'Look, my darling,' said Miss Winter. 'It's my most recent painting of the Ward's nephews.' It was on an easel in the middle of the room.

Oh my God. No!

'Such beautiful Twins.'

Sam and Jack.

I stumbled back, two, three, four steps, until I bumped

against a cabinet and my left hand shot out for balance and knocked over a vase. A Hintersea-shaped puddle formed next to flowers that grow in the fields near Compton – flowers of the same type as those on Will's grave.

'You lied,' I mumbled, barely audible. 'It was you who put the flowers there, not Mike.'

'Something said to achieve a Challenge is never a lie,' Miss Winter said.

I fell to the floor and saw two walking sticks guide feet towards my head.

Miss Winter held up my head so that I could see a man bend towards me. For a moment I thought that it was The Twins' father.

'Hello, my dear Ben. My name is Tobias Thatcher, Games Master. I am the direct descendant of the Ward of Hintersea. You will have to learn the honour and responsibility of that position.'

I tried to clamber away, to slide towards the stairs.

'More tea?' laughed Miss Winter. '*Darling?*'

Tobias Thatcher's dark brown eyes captivated me. 'I know that you've met my twin brother,' he said, ponderously. 'And his *splendid* twin sons.' He smiled. 'Sam and Jack are *marvellous*, aren't they? Just like my brother and me when we were young.'

I groaned for help.

'No one will hear you,' he said as he stood upright, holding his back. 'I gather you're now a Challenger, as you should be.' Each word seemed carefully considered, almost laboured. 'You should be happy to be here, where you belong.'

What I said came out as a gurgle.

'If you close your eyes, you will find out where the others went. I promise,' he said. 'Go on, close your eyes. . .'

I didn't want to; but I couldn't help it. My head touched the floor.

'I want to paint him again, right now,' said Mrs Winter.

The bubbles in front of my eyes grew bigger and bigger until one engulfed me. Everything went silent and black.

TWO DAYS TO GO

✏️ Draft Email

To:	Carolineterm95
Cc:	
Subject:	The Past

Hi Caroline

Someone else has to know the whole truth.

'Christmas Eve, 2016. The middle of London, next to Big Ben. Midday,' he said. Then I watched him disappear into the woodland. With anyone else, they'd be empty words.

It was so far in the future I thought we'd never get here.

I came close to telling you everything when we went to Compton for Gran's funeral. You mentioned the view from the houses in Compton across Lake Hintersea and how it must be full of memories. 'Yeah,' I said. Just *Yeah* – not *I can remember what we did as if it was yesterday.* Not *I can remember the faces of those who died.*

Someone else has to know the truth in case it all goes wrong.

I'm not sure when it all started to change. Maybe that night at the party. It was the first time I'd set out to hurt someone else.

Now you see why I have a dog, despite the hassle that Ewok is. And you understand why he had to be a Leavitt Bulldog.

I still have all the documents from the story – they're here in my bedroom in a small black metal case bound up with brown tape. You'll know it when you see it.

I can't believe this is about me. Please read the whole thing before judging me. I want you to know all of it.

I know you'll understand. You were there.

I'm going |

NOVEMBER 2011
BEYOND DEATH

I hazily remember being moved. The Twins were there, so was Mr Thatcher. Miss Winter's voice gabbled in the background. But all I wanted to do was relax, close my eyes, and drift back to oblivion.

I awoke with a start with no idea of time or location. The shouting I heard was mine.

'Keep it down. There's no *point*. I've tried. I've done nothing but try.' It was Blake – thick glasses, corduroy trousers, shirt with a collar. Alive and apparently unharmed.

'Oh my God,' I said. 'You're safe! You're here.' For a fleeting moment I was actually pleased. Then the awful obvious truth hit me. We were both chained to metal beds by one hand. The mattresses were basic; there were no sheets.

'I *tried* to warn you that they were trouble. I tried! I *really* tried. But you wouldn't listen. It was all about *you* . . . And now look what's happened. I tried to tell you but you were thick in the head. Thick in the head.' Blake pressed thin lips together and pointed aggressively at his temple with one finger.

'I know. I know. Blake, you were right and I was wrong.' I rubbed my eyes. 'Oh God – I can't believe how wrong I've been. I suppose I was hoping for . . .' I thought of Will.

Blake's teeth were pressed hard together and his eyes bore into me. 'I tried to warn you, but you wouldn't listen, and now look where we are. We're going to die – before our lives have even begun.' He turned his head away from me, empty of hope.

'I know I've messed up,' I whispered. 'I *know* I've been stupid. Please look at me.'

Blake slowly turned back. His eyes were bloodshot.

'But, look, we haven't woken up dead, have we? We're still alive for a reason,' I said. Would they actually hurt me? 'The Twins always have a reason.'

'Yeah,' Blake mumbled. He breathed out heavily, letting his shoulders and head fall. 'That's what worries me. Might be better if they'd just killed us at the start.'

I studied the room, a red brick cellar that smelt of urine. My bed was opposite a solid metal door and to my left, little more than six feet away, was Blake's bed. There was a video camera in the top right corner. The cellar might have been that of a thousand houses around the country, but the door was purpose-built and slightly dented and scratched at the level a kick would land. We were not the first to be held here. 'Where the hell are we?'

'I'm not sure. Underground. There's no noise.' His voice was low and grim. 'There's no way out.'

'Help!' I shouted. Even louder: 'Help! Let us out!'

'I've *tried* that,' he shouted. 'I've tried it for all of yesterday and the day before and . . .' He looked away. 'I already can't remember how long I've been here. That light never goes off.'

'Have they said anything? Are they going to . . .' My sentence faded away to nothing.

'I don't know,' Blake said. He leaned across towards me, as far as he could. 'But I'm scared. They're not right in the head. They're not normal.'

I looked at the room again, with a magician's eye. People had been locked inside milk churns, buried underground, wrapped up in chains – a good magician could always find his way out. But the video camera made me swear under my breath. I noticed a bottle of water and an empty plastic plate by Blake's bed. On the other side there was a plastic bucket, probably where the smell was coming from. There was an identical one within my reach. 'Who brought this stuff?'

'He said he was Jack, but I can't tell.' Blake stared at me. 'I won't ever go mad, you know that. I won't go mad.' He started to cry. He was going mad already.

'We're both going to get outta here,' I said, though didn't believe it for a second. The world was a Game to The Twins: that was what they had been told from birth: there were no limits: everything was a *Challenge*.

I looked at the lock on the door. 'Does he use a key?'

'Yes.'

I bit my tongue in thought.

Blake continued: 'A key. And I think there's a bolt.'

No magician, no matter how clever, can undo a bolt that's on the far side of a door. No magician can do *real* magic. I strained at the chain and tried to move the bed, but it was screwed to the floor.

Without the sound of approaching footsteps, we heard a bolt slid back, then another, and a key turn in the lock. Sam and Jack strutted in.

They weren't wearing masks. I had vaguely hoped that Blake had *assumed* it was Sam and Jack, but they were open about their identity. I knew what that meant: they were never going to let Blake leave alive. Me? *Maybe* – I couldn't be sure how their logic was working. Perhaps, just perhaps, they still felt I was unable to report them without incriminating myself. But if they killed Blake? That would change the balance. Unless that was something they wanted to pin on me?

'I want to know why I'm here! I haven't done anything to hurt you!' Blake squealed. 'My parents don't have any money.' He still hoped this was a straightforward kidnapping.

The Twins looked down at Blake dismissively.

My words came out as a growl. 'Is this just for fun, or because of a Challenge?'

'Ben.' Sam shook his head. 'You need to chill, man.' (Yes – *You need to chill*: that's exactly what he said.) 'You're only chained because we knew you wouldn't be calm. We don't want you to be uncomfortable.'

'Spare me this shit,' I said. 'You're just a couple of weirdos.'

Jack draped his arm round his brother's shoulders. 'We're chess players.' He laughed.

I spat on the floor. It was the first thing that came into my head as a way to show disgust. 'Don't be mental – I'm a human being, not some sort of play *object*.' I swore at them.

'Ben, Ben . . . you don't get it, do you?' Sam moved closer. 'You don't appreciate how my uncle has watched you – how we have *all* watched you. The Games Master studied you as a baby when you were looked after by your grandmother. He observed your first steps down your path; he saw the first time the stabilizers came off your bike. He saw you on the day that Will left. You're the star of the show.'

Blake screamed for help towards the open door. 'Let me out of here,' he yelled. 'Let me out! Help!'

As Jack put his hand round his throat, Blake's voice became a gargle and then, as the squeezing intensified, a croak. I thought he was going to strangle him.

'Blake – keep quiet!' I shouted. 'Jack, please let him go!'

Jack slowly released his grip. 'You need to be careful,' he said into Blake's ear. 'You're nothing – you're just a prop. We could kill you and replace you with someone else, just like that!' He snapped his fingers in front of Blake's nose.

Blake wheezed and put his free hand to his reddened neck. 'You leave me alone, you bully!'

'You're complete psychos,' I said. 'Both of you.'

Sam chuckled – not a crazy laugh, but the sound of water running over rocks. 'We're not idiots who've played too many first-person shooter games. We're special. We're supermen. We can do anything. We're as different to the likes of him –' he pointed at Blake – 'as a lion is to a slug.'

'And what about me?' I asked.

Sam came over and sat on the bed next to me. It happened quickly, before I could brace myself to resist. He put his arm around me, his hand on my head, and pulled me so that my cheek was against his chest. 'You're special,' he said. 'You're one of us.'

'I'm nothing like you,' I said.

Jack came to the other side of the bed. 'You're very much like us. You're more like us than you believe.'

I told him to f-off and let us go. The Twins had changed me: I wasn't a timid boy to be cowed.

'How much do you know about your mother?' asked Sam.

'You just keep her out of this,' I growled. I swore in the strongest way I could, but hurling insults didn't make me feel better.

Sam ignored me and carried on. 'She used to work at Lakeside House.'

'Yeah . . .' I didn't like where this was going.

'She was a bit of a babe,' said Jack, standing up.

'And the Games Master liked her,' said Sam, also standing. 'He liked her very much. And she liked him. And nine months later you came along.'

'No, that's total bollocks,' I said despondently. I looked

at The Twins' eyes: slightly darker brown than mine. Their hair: lighter, just. Then I started to laugh: it was the weirdest thing, a sort of exaggerated, uncontrolled, hysterical giggling, even though I didn't find anything remotely funny.

Jack seemed annoyed. 'We're related. Pretty funny, eh?' It was the first time I'd actually irritated him.

My mind was like a runaway carriage struggling to stay on railway tracks. I thought of the mother I knew from pictures: a mother with striking blue eyes I hadn't inherited. I wondered if my grandmother was aware. 'It's not true,' I insisted. Stupidly, into my head came *Star Wars* and Luke Skywalker and Darth Vader.

Blake's breathing was fast and his eyes flitted around the room.

'And that brings us to our Challenge,' said Sam. 'And it's also a test.'

'What?' I said. 'I don't get it.' I glanced at Blake. 'Why is he here?'

Jack looked at Blake dismissively and said: 'Sorry, mate. It had to be someone.'

The Twins returned about three or four hours later with pasta and water. I was frantically thirsty and gulped down nearly all the water in one go. But I didn't finish the bottle – I wanted it in case the cap was useful to turn the screws that held down the bed. Next time, a full bottle might be used to smash the light or, possibly, disable the video camera. Anything was worth a try.

I thanked The Twins for bringing the food. They were clever – but not so clever that they knew what was going on in my head. Their trust might gain me a tiny advantage. 'No one else needs to get hurt,' I said.

'This isn't about Blake, and it wasn't about Mike, or even *Will*,' Sam said. 'Don't you understand? This is about *you*!' He waved his hands towards me as if he were introducing the star of the show.

Sam said: 'The Games Master said: "I Challenge you to make an innocent person kill an innocent person." We had to tease it out, like a game of chess.'

Jack added: 'We thought it was the *ultimate* Challenge, especially when we decided to involve our innocent cousin, the one that the Games Master had carefully watched grow up. It was more than a Challenge. It was a chance to bring you into the family.'

'What the hell are you talking about?' said Blake. 'You're sick in the head. All of you!' He glared at me as well. 'Including you!' For a few seconds the only sound was the clanking of Blake tugging on his handcuff chain.

'I still don't understand why we're here now,' I said, searching for the twisted logic.

Sam went down on his haunches on the side of my bed away from Blake. 'Ben, you can walk out of here any time you like.' He pointed at the open door. 'There you go: you can fly out, free as a bird. The Games Master is desperate to see you. He has said that one day you could become the Challenge Setter. You can live in Timberline or Lakeside House as one of the family, as soon as you prove that you're one of us.'

'You know I want to leave right now.' I didn't break his gaze.

'In that case,' said Sam. 'You just have to inject Blake with this.' He stepped outside and returned with a syringe held up as if it were a sacred sword. He placed it on the floor next to my bed, stepped back, and smiled.

'What's in the syringe?' I asked.

'Already tempted?' chuckled Sam. Everything was a Game.

Blake spoke quickly through tears in a high pitched voice: 'We-want-to-know-what's-in-the-bloody-syringe!'

'Tetrodotoxin,' said Jack. 'From the blue-ringed octopus.

Probably the fastest poison around. Just that little bit will paralyse you, stop your breathing and heart, quick as a flash. Simple. Painless. Easy. There's enough for one.' He pointed his index finger and winked, first at me, then at Blake.

Blake pulled his knees to him as far away from me as possible and repeated, 'Oh no! Oh no!'

For a time I didn't say anything. I considered grabbing the syringe and trying to drive it into Sam's neck – but I would never have been able to pick it up and lunge at him quickly enough, even if I could reach, and I certainly didn't have the strength to overwhelm him, even without his brother getting involved.

I stared at the long hypodermic needle. 'Are you kidding? And if I don't? What if I just spray the contents over the wall?'

'If you don't co-operate,' said Jack, 'you're not worthy to join the family, and you'll both stay in this room, for ever and ever and ever . . . Of course, if anything should happen to the Thatchers, then you would be in trouble . . .' He shrugged. 'No one would ever find you here.'

'You can't keep us chained to a bed,' Blake whined.

Sam spat: 'This isn't a hotel. You're just a piece on a chessboard that will get enough food and water to stay alive. You'll have to piss and shit in a bucket and be grateful that we'll empty it.'

Jack: 'There'll be no luxuries. Nothing at all. Ever.'

I stared at the needle. 'And what if I inject myself?'

'Then we will have misjudged the power of the blood that runs through your veins,' said Sam. 'And we will have no use for Blake.'

'Either way, I'm dead!' wailed Blake. He stuck his hand in his mouth in an attempt to stop his own noise.

'We'll make sure that the rules of the Game are followed,' said Jack. 'Don't underestimate us. Our family has been playing Games and Challenges for centuries.' He pointed at the camera. 'We'll be watching.'

Jack then held me down, my face buried in my mattress. I tried to struggle, but couldn't move an inch. To begin with, I had no idea why, but then heard the jangling of a chain. When I was allowed to raise my head, I saw that I was now handcuffed to a chain that was about six feet long. They had given me enough room to reach Blake.

Without another word, Sam stood up and walked out, and Jack closed the door behind him. There was the scrape of bolts being drawn across.

'I've heard of tetrodotoxin,' wittered Blake. 'I reckon it *does* come from an octopus.' He was pale and shaking.

'You're going to kill me eventually, aren't you? You're going to end up just like them.'

I turned my back to the camera and spoke quietly. I hardly recognized my own voice: 'You need to calm down and do what I say. Otherwise I really will stick this needle up your arse.' I tried to look as sincere as I could. 'They may not get this, but I'll never hurt you, I promise.' I looked at the syringe. 'I'm not like that.'

NOVEMBER 2011
DEATH

I doubted that we could play the long game and hope The Twins became slack captors over time. Even without the massive limitations imposed by twenty-four-hour surveillance, we wouldn't be tunnelling out behind a poster of Rita Hayworth. It was more likely that the rules of the Challenge would change against us. Somehow, we would have to leave through the door.

'Don't say anything,' I whispered. I tugged at my ear on the far side of the camera to suggest we were being listened to. 'Don't look at that camera – or that.' I shot my eyes towards the syringe.

'OK, OK, you're in charge,' said Blake.

He had to understand. 'Whenever we talk, look at my face and try to forget where we are,' I insisted.

He nodded and forced out the flicker of a smile. 'OK.'

I had never known The Twins make a mistake before. But they had made two.

Without cutting, there was no way to remove the chain from the metal structure of the bed; and it's impossible to slide a tight handcuff over your hand (even dislocating your thumb doesn't work). But with a flat piece of metal, a shim, it's easy to get out of regulation handcuffs: I'd done it a hundred times. A paperclip could do the job – or, in theory, though I'd never tried it, the needle of a syringe.

The Twins' Mistake Number One: giving me the tools.

And their second mistake?

Never give a magician something to work behind. A curtain, a box – any sort of shield. Even a bed. And the syringe had been placed on the side of the bed nearest Blake, away from the camera.

The Twins were human. I shuddered to think that some of their blood might run through me.

If I'd stopped to think, it might have taken me days to find the courage to act. But I wasn't 'Will's shadow' any more.

I pressed my finger to my lips and sat on the side of the bed facing Blake, the camera behind me, and quickly scooped the syringe off the floor with my left hand as I adjusted my position.

Blake hissed, 'No! Don't—'

I tapped my finger to my lips and stared at him. 'I need to have a conversation with you,' I said. 'You need

236

to talk to me. Look straight at me.' I moved my right hand in rhythm with my words, aware that I might be being watched – and with my left hand tried to remove the needle from the syringe. 'Blake, tell me how you feel.'

Blake chuntered away about how terrified he was, how I was going to get fed up and kill him, how his body would be buried in an unmarked grave somewhere in a forest.

I worked on the needle. I imagined it sliding out or unclipping, but it was welded to the plastic and I had to twist and turn in a way that would have made Uri Geller proud. I couldn't risk more than a very occasional glance at what I was doing. A few times I nicked my finger or the palm of my hand with the end of the needle and resisted the burning temptation to stop and have a look . . .

Eventually I held in my left hand one plastic syringe and one metal needle.

Now it was a race against time to act before The Twins returned.

You might think that the clever part was to twist the needle into shape – or to know how to insert it, key-like, into the handcuffs and make them pop open. That was just knowledge. The real sweat was to be able to do this calmly and quickly, and in short bursts so that my arms weren't ever behind my back for long. I had to keep my breathing steady. It's the best bit of magic I have ever done in my life.

Blake had to remain chained. Even if I could have invisibly crossed the room, I had to think like a magician. Deception and distraction. Make the audience look the wrong way.

There was a terrifying, exhilarating moment when the handcuff popped open.

Annoyingly, the needle was so bent that there was no way I could put it back into the syringe to make a weapon. Perhaps Blake could somehow drive the blunt syringe into one of The Twins while I grappled with the other. Maybe I could get out and . . . No. I would have to lock both of The Twins in the room with Blake and dash for help.

'Do you have a plan?' Blake asked.

'Yes,' I said. 'Just grab hold of the nearest Twin and don't let go.'

For several hours, we sat in silence. There was nothing to say. No grand speeches for fear of being overheard. I just went over and over it all in my head, wondering if there were any little advantages we could gain.

Eventually, we heard bolts slide back . . .

I quickly threw Blake the syringe. 'Threaten to stab yourself,' I hissed.

. . . and the door opened.

I had been desperately hoping that only one of The Twins would arrive – but they were both there. Sam came in first, taking the keys out of the door as he did.

Jack followed with two lasagnes in black-plastic microwave containers: 'Sorry, guys, no cutlery,' were his first words. *Sorry, guys, no cutlery* – as if we were all mates together on a camping trip. He really didn't understand that we were normal human beings who didn't want to play this evil game. It was the desensitized mind-set of the prison camp guard.

I stared at Blake and shouted: 'No – don't do it! Give it back!'

Blake started screaming: 'I can't bear this any longer – I've had enough! I've had enough!' The stress of the situation produced a terrifyingly realistic performance. The syringe was held to his stomach, apparently with the needle already in, but the plunger not pressed.

The Twins were unlike anyone else I have ever known, but they responded for a split second in the way that anyone would: they looked towards the action. Maybe they didn't really care if Blake stabbed himself – but they looked. There isn't a magician in the world that doesn't rely on this impulse.

Sam went over to him and Jack bent down to put the lasagnes on the floor. It was a natural response – and exactly what I needed.

I leaped up and was pulling the door closed – as hard as I could – in a second. Had it been anyone else, I would have had it shut, held it, and pulled the bolt across, but Jack thrust his arm in the way. It was another instant of remarkable quick thinking. With the force I was using to pull metal into metal, with sharp right angles on both, I would have snapped his fingers off, but the door rebounded off his arm.

Then a moment that changed everything: Jack's left hand went to his right arm, midway between elbow and wrist, and he looked down for a second. My fist arrived with all the force that I could muster. It was Desperation multiplied by Anger multiplied by Revenge.

Fear returned as I ran away down an unknown passageway.

I saw blood explode at right angles from Sam's face and, for a split second, Jack's leg being held on to by Blake, who may have been a stick-man but held on for precious, vital, desperate seconds until he was knocked unconscious. (I have to add that Blake now only has 20 per cent hearing in his left ear after the battering he took.)

I was determined to hurtle down the passageway with the risk that I would spiral out of control if I slipped. I passed two rooms; then there were stone steps to the left with a door at the top.

I emerged into another room that was like an underground shed. I saw an old motor and small blue barrels and wooden slats from a rowing boat. Possibly a weapon? No – I couldn't risk a direct fight.

The only way out seemed to be a metal ladder that rose vertically in the far right-hand corner of the room, and I ran over and started climbing, forcing my hands and legs to work methodically and quickly, unaware whether the ceiling hatch above would open.

There was a trapdoor that swung up and I clambered out into a large shed, next to a trailer that held *Evening Cloud*. I glanced down and saw one of the Twins, from the blood on his face I presume it was Sam, about to ascend the metal ladder.

It took me two or three frantic seconds to realize that there was no way I could manoeuvre the trailer in place to hold the door shut, so I burst out into the damp, dark air, skidding past a parked Land Rover.

I had three choices. Down the hill towards the road: surely the best and logical option – certainly the fastest route to the road and a passing car. To the right, away from Timberline and further into the woods: probably the best place to hide. To the left, towards Timberline.

I immediately went left. Yes, left – towards the lair, and possibly towards their father and who-knows-what else.

After I turned the corner out of sight of the boat shed, I heard the Land Rover trundle away from me, down the hill, a glinting light searching in the trees. Sam must have been at the wheel.

As soon as my head turned, I saw lights coming towards me, beaming into the air as they approached the brow of the hill. There was no choice but to throw myself left, down the slope, into the undergrowth. Arms to my side, I buried my face in the mud.

The Mercedes, I presume driven by Mr Thatcher, squelched past, flicking specks of mud over the edge and on to my head. I thought of how it all started with a spinning wheel firing mud at Will.

My lungs were bursting and calf muscles rock-solid as I reached Timberline. Perhaps I could hear car engines in the distance, or it might have been the wind droning through the trees. The house was dark and silent. Empty?

The nearest phone was inside.

I put my elbow through the glass in one of the old-fashioned twelve-pane windows, cutting my hand with a Z-shaped slice as I eased back the latch. The rumbling and squeaking of the window sounded like Bullseye's bark – but no one was looking for me here. A smudge of blood in the shape of the letter T was left on the door.

My muddy footsteps made their way to the most unlikely place: the nearest telephone was in Mr Thatcher's study.

Dialling tone.

999.

Police.

Help.

Come quickly.

The portrait of the Ward of Hintersea – Games Master of yesteryear – stared down at me.

Missing boy.

Captive.

Possible murder.

A police car passing along the main road at the head of the valley was sent racing towards Timberline.

I hid at the back of the house in the trees until pale blue emergency lights dimly lit the trees and I heard police radios. Then I edged round the side of the house and, hoarsely pleading for help, waving my arms frantically, I ran towards the nearest policeman.

Early the next morning, when the police came to Lakeside House, and Mrs Winter told the Games Master, allegedly my birth father, that the police were waiting downstairs, a shotgun blast rang out and his blood was seen against the windows of the Lantern Room. I felt no sense of loss and never have. I've never tried to confirm that he was actually my father. I'm happy to doubt that The Twins were my cousins.

I heard a few weeks later that Lakeside House was mine. A prize that brought no joy. If 'Mr Winter' thought it brought obligations, he was wrong.

There were multiple arrests and weeks of forensic unpicking. The remains of a man who went missing in 1968 were discovered in the Timberline woods. Mr Thatcher insisted that he knew nothing about that – he would only have been sixteen at the time.

Waist-high weeds stand like guards on the drive.

Timberline sits empty.

Jack was never found.

And that is where the story officially ends.

*

But I want to be honest about what *really* happened.

When I opened the door of Mr Thatcher's study to hide in the trees outside I saw headlights shine through the glass in the front door and down the hallway.

I crept forwards and then peered out of the window to the right. Sam was partially hidden, standing in front of the Land Rover, infrared binoculars searching for me from the best vantage point.

The engine of the Land Rover ticked over; I eased open the front door of the house.

Hidden behind the vehicle, I tiptoed my way forward, desperate not to make a noise on the gravel. The slightest hint of a police siren echoed up the valley as I crouched down and peered around the side.

Sam scanned with the binoculars.

I ran, fast. It was between the second and third strides – of five – that I heard Jack's voice shout from my left.

'Behind!'

Sam turned as I arrived and threw my weight into him. I don't understand why he didn't stop himself if he could. Perhaps he truly thought he was indestructible. He went over the edge, silently, gracefully, head between his arms like a diver. I think he glanced at me. Branches were beaten off trees as he fell and then I heard a dull thud.

His body was not discovered at the bottom of the cliff: he was found at the end of a bloody trail two hundred yards into the lower woods. The police supposed that Jack had moved him. They didn't know The Twins.

I fell to the ground a few inches short of the drop, then stood up to see sirens and blue lights turning the corner into the Timberline drive.

Jack looked towards the blue lights and then me. He took four paces forward and I readied myself to run. Instead, he said, solemnly: 'You will never know when we're going to come and get you. Worry every night that we'll come in your sleep. If not before, we'll see you on Christmas Eve, 2016. The middle of London, next to Big Ben. Midday.' The sirens were loud now, nearly at the top of the drive. 'Be there – or we *will* find you.'

Jack ran into the woodland and I ran back into the house, to return seconds later as the police Volvo drew up on the gravel outside Timberline.

A FEW HOURS TO GO

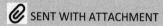 Sent Email

To:	Carolineterm95
Cc:	
Subject:	The Past

@ SENT WITH ATTACHMENT

Hi Caroline

Someone else has to know the whole truth.

'Christmas Eve, 2016. The middle of London, next to Big Ben. Midday,' he said. Then I watched him disappear into the woodland. With anyone else, they'd be empty words.

It was so far in the future I thought we'd never get here.

I came close to telling you everything when we went to Compton for Gran's funeral. You mentioned the view from the houses in Compton across Lake Hintersea and how it must be full of memories. 'Yeah,' I said. Just *Yeah* – not *I can remember what we did as if it was yesterday.* Not *I can remember the faces of those who died.*

Someone else has to know the truth in case it all goes wrong.

I'm not sure when it all started to change. Maybe that night at the party. It was the first time I'd set out to hurt someone else.

Now you see why I have a dog, despite the hassle that Ewok is. And you understand why he had to be a Leavitt Bulldog.

I still have all the documents from the story – they're here in my bedroom in a small black metal case bound up with brown tape. You'll know it when you see it.

I can't believe this is about me. Please read the whole thing before judging me. I want you to know all of it.

I know you'll understand. You were there.

I'm going to meet Jack. You wonder why I'm not going to the police?

I'm going to punish him for what he did to Will and to Mike and to Blake and to others. And to me. There – now you know the whole story.

No one will be sorry. No one who really knows him.

If not – if you go to the police – I'll take whatever justice has for me.

With my love,

Ben

AFTER THE MEETING WITH JACK

✉ Sent Email

To:	Carolineterm95
Cc:	
Subject:	Right now

To Caroline:

I thought you'd like to know what happened earlier today.

I left home about eleven this morning and caught the Tube. I like the Tube – all of those lives coming together like little trickles of water and pouring into a great river. A torrent. The closer people come together, the less they notice one another.

I took a weapon with me, just in case. What sort of weapon do you think it was? Candlestick? Knife? Revolver? Rope? Poison?

I wanted to keep my promise. Christmas Eve, 2016. The middle of London, next to Big Ben. Midday. Not empty words.

He stood out from the crowd. The same hawk-like appearance. He didn't see me. I look different now.

The homeless woman told him to go down to the river, by the statue of Boudicca. The man there told him to get on the boat to Greenwich. I arranged all that.

I was sure he was alone.

I met him at Greenwich.

Jack.

Hi, Ben.

We stared at one another for a minute.

Why did you come? I was going to give nothing away, in case he was wired – the same trick as on the lake.

He wanted me to come here, to his fancy riverside flat bought with Lakeside House money. To talk.

But he had other plans. He told me he had written to you.

Ben always was different. One of us.

I'm going to take his laptop and destroy it. I hope you enjoy reading the story he has written. Interesting how he saw it.

I'd keep quiet, if I were you.

It would be an easy **Challenge** to come for you. I remember you well.

Ben can't come to the computer right now. He's a bit tied up and can't seem to move too well.

What do you think I should do with my cousin?

Maybe leave him for another five years?

Maybe not.

Kisses,

Jack

ABOUT THE AUTHOR

Tom Hoyle is the pseudonym of a London head teacher.

ACKNOWLEDGEMENTS

Thank you to all who have helped *The Challenge* reach the page, especially those who have been there since Book One – three wonderful ladies: AW (from that soaking-wet day onwards), Venetia Gosling at Macmillan and Gillie Russell at Aitken Alexander. Thank you also to CH and CP for confirming that the story had mileage. And thank you very much to Macmillan editor Lucy Pearse (wisdom and tolerance – and the most essential person to *The Challenge*), cover designer Rachel Vale (great, again), Jess Rigby and Kat McKenna (for organizing marketing), and Catherine Alport (for arranging publicity).

THIRTEEN

TOM HOYLE

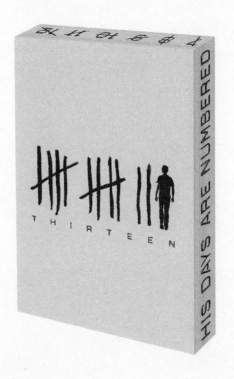

THEY'RE DYING
ONE BY ONE.

SPIDERS

TOM HOYLE

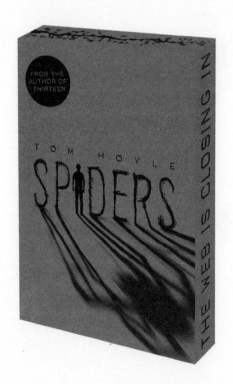

THEY'LL MAKE YOUR SKIN CRAWL.

SURVIVOR

TOM HOYLE

NOBODY IS SAFE.